THE OTHER FACE OF MURDER

A Novel
By
Gil Porat

ALONDRA PRESS, LLC

Published by Alondra Press
www.alondrapress.com
lark@alondrapress.com

Copyright © 2008 by Gil Porat

All rights reserved. No part of this publication may be reproduced or transmitted in any form or by any means without permission from the publisher, except for brief passages in connection with a review.

The Other Face of Murder
By Gil Porat

ISBN 978-0-9814523-1-9
Library of Congress CIP No. 2008920161
Printed on acid-free paper in the United States

Cover Design by Art Republic of Texas

For information write to
ALONDRA PRESS, LLC
10122 Shadow Wood # 19
Houston, TX 77043

If you are unable to order this book from your local bookseller, you may order directly from the publisher, at www.alondrapress.com or at lark@alondrapress.com

**Dedicated to those laboring to dignify
the future dead.**

ONE

My best buddy, Earl Haynes, was the first to arrive for the dinner party. Earl looked like the college lineman who is just a little out of shape. He was a jovial type who appealed to women who like cuddly, teddy-bear physiques. Having a flattened abdomen was something he desired, but watching workout tapes while eating never produced recognizable results. His slightly crooked nose, a souvenir from his high-school wrestling days, rescued him from the banality of a classic pretty-boy face.

Other than his rustic attire, he had adapted to the big city remarkably well, given that the water tower was the tallest structure in his hometown of Reform, Alabama. Reform was so small, he'd tell us, that people only gave out the last four digits of their phone numbers because the first three digits were the same for everyone. He left the place a decade ago to attend medical school, but retained a slight southern drawl, and much of the town's character. The thing about Earl was that it didn't matter where he was. Wherever he was, he felt at home. It's a quality I envied.

You wouldn't have even noticed his accent much except for the fact that his whole body emitted southern culture. Not the style of the courtly, southern gentleman. Rather, a tough rugged guy who drove a red pick-up truck, and listened to Lynyrd Skynyrd and the Allman Brothers - that sort of thing. He believed the three most important years in American history were 1492, 1776, and 2001 (not because of September 11, but for the loss of Dale Earnhardt on the last lap of the Daytona 500 that year). Be that as it may, to oversimplify Earl would mistakenly veil an astonishingly complex mind.

I was glad Earl came ahead of the other guests. We hadn't seen each other since he passed out at my house two weeks prior to the dinner party. On that occasion, we required a taxi to haul us home from a downtown bar to my place. When we got home, he had made his wobbly way over to my baby grand to ogle one of the carelessly framed photos on top of the seldom-played piano. "Hey, Karen has always been a good looking girl in my eyes," he said, "but these pictures make her look totally great." At which point I swore at him and explained he was actually looking at a picture of my mother taken two decades ago. "Well, is she still married?" he asked, not missing a beat.

"She's an aging widow on the verge of losing her marbles. If one more difficult life circumstance emerges, she might just transform into one of those crazy ladies who collects every stray cat in the neighborhood. Stay away from her."

Earl always arrived at his host's home carting a twelve-pack of McTarnahans Ale. Actually, he arrived just about anywhere carrying McTarnahans Ale. He was not an alcoholic, but certainly drank to a greater degree than the average person. He claimed that he didn't drink to relax, but rather to make other people more interesting. Our colleagues at the hospital joked that Earl rarely made a diagnosis of alcoholism because patients could only be diagnosed as alcoholics if they were heavier drinkers than their doctor. He knew the health risks of alcohol, but like most physicians he found ways to justify his hang-ups. *It's true alcohol kills brain cells, but only the wimpy ones*, he'd profess.

Earl's stellar reputation as a compassionate, brilliant oncologist hadn't led to a case of high self-regard. Among friends he sometimes despaired that his job was to poison already dying patients. When medical breakthroughs arrive that will eventually make chemotherapy obsolete, it will be a relief to him, even if it means being out of a job. Like most people, he desired respect, but Earl never cared what venue that respect came in. Whether he was a happy hour hero, or oncologist to the elite, it didn't matter to him.

As usual, Earl had left all remnants of his professional demeanor at the hospital. He carried the ale into the kitchen and began describing some long-legged girl he saw at the convenience store on the way to my house.

"Maaa-an, you should have seen her. I felt like dropping protein right on that there spot."

Luckily the doorbell rang, sparing me from hearing further details. Our friend Roy stood on the porch, shifting from one foot to the other.

Roy's sandy blond hair hung just below his shoulders. He was a nerdy guy, and it never bothered him. Being a software programmer surrounded him with fellow unabashed geeks who repelled cool. Sci-fi books, comics, and classic rock were his passions. He arrived wearing green corduroy pants and a blue t-shirt with a red and yellow Superman symbol on the chest. Roy always wore t-shirts one size too small. That way he could show off the barbed wire tattoo that encircled his right bicep. People with that tattoo usually have well built muscles. But Roy had never worked out a day in his life. Something about him always reminded me of Shaggy from the old Scooby-Doo cartoons.

Roy sat down on the couch and immediately started fidgeting with his hands and rambling about the craziness of his day.

"It all started this morning. Well, actually it started last night. I went camping at the coast with my buddy, Potter. We woke up after a night of rain, and discovered we were basically sleeping in a frozen puddle," said Roy.

"That's no way to greet the new day," I acknowledged.

"Yeah, well that was just the start of it. We decided to pack up and head for the car. When we got to the car, we both realized we didn't bring a change of clothes. Man, we were soaked."

"Bummer," I said halfheartedly.

"Yeah, so we decided to strip and headed back to Portland naked, but dry," he said, crossing and then uncrossing his legs. Roy's posture was uncomfortable to observe. His left shoulder was always a few inches lower than the right. No wonder he often complained of back pain.

"Nothing like feeling dry," I said, thinking that was the end of the story. Somewhat fruity, but understandable given the circumstances they were in.

"Yeah, and we drove back pretty fast. We passed this slow Chevrolet on the road. Wouldn't you know it, a mile later we're at a stop sign in Tillamook and the damn Chevrolet rear ends us."

"Oh gosh," I mumbled, hoping my intonation sounded like one of concern, rather than one of amusement. In truth, I was internally grinning, just sitting back, amused by Roy's narration. The ambience in the room reminded me of Thoreau's Walden Pond. This was the stuff he was writing about, albeit an entire coast away: The simple and ordinary pleasure of good, intimate conversation with friends, neighbors, and loved ones. Roy continued his story, twisting a strand of his long hair between his thumb and index finger as he spoke.

"Yeah, so Potter and I got out of the car to get our soaked clothes from the trunk. But, wouldn't you know it, the Chevrolet had smashed in our trunk and it wouldn't open."

Earl and I chuckled. Roy, not amused, paused until we simmered down, then resumed his narrative. "So there we were, on a chilly morning, standing naked in the middle of the road. As fate would have it, there was a church on the same corner as the stop sign. It was called Truth or Consequences Church of Christ. The congregation heard the crash, and everyone poured outside to see if we needed help.

"Twenty minutes later we were sitting with towels around our waists in the Tillamook police station. The cop was acting like a real jerk. One of the first things he did when he arrested us was take our watches. He put them in a desk drawer filled with tons of other watches. You know, I never got my watch back."

Earl guffawed. Beer came out his nose. "You two gone and got yourselves in quite the predicament," he said.

Roy, recognizing he had enthralled his audience with the hilarity of it all, continued. "I was scared shitless. Seriously, I really had to go to the bathroom. The cop eventually let me use the restroom. No kidding man, I ended up clogging the toilet. It was the biggest and smelliest crap-out I've ever had. Luckily, Potter had paid the fine on his credit card while I was in the bathroom. When I got out of the bathroom I was just about to tell the cop about the toilet, when he told me I was free to go. Knowing there was only one cop car in town and that it was at the police station, we bolted out of town like bats out of hell – still only wrapped with towels around our waists."

I became concerned. Not about Roy, but that Earl was going to get beer on my carpet via his nose. He surprised me when he began to chide Roy. "I never understood why people allow heavy toilet buildup. If you just took a big crap and you know there's another load on the way, then flush the damn toilet! You know the next droppings could end up clogging the throne. A clogged toilet is the awfullest thing. It doesn't make sense to ever risk that happening."

Roy may not have been done with his story, but by that time Grant and his girlfriend, Tarini, had arrived. Tarini was a lovely half-Hindu, half-American doctor of internal medicine whom Grant had met shortly after divorcing his wife. I was happy to see they made it to our house; earlier that morning, Grant had telephoned to say he might be coming down with the flu. The germ of his disease turned out to be his secretary. She had negligently brewed decaffeinated coffee for his mandatory morning cup, causing his soul to remain in hibernation until his observant nurse discovered the empty decaf bag in the waste basket.

I had met Grant a few years ago, soon after I arrived in the city to join Portland Premier Health Partners. His medical practice rented space in the same office building as my group. Right off, he invited me to his wife's (now ex-wife's) birthday party. They would be celebrating at a "topless" bar, he told me. I was keyed up at the prospect because it seemed I was the only guy on earth who by age thirty-four hadn't been to a strip-club. In anticipation, I went to the bank to get fifty dollars in singles. What a letdown when I got to the party and realized we were at a "tapas" bar. The tasty array of Spanish "small-plates" was no consolation prize. Not to mention the embarrassment of using forty-three single dollars to pay for my portion of the bill.

Realizing she was late, Karen had dressed quickly, and raced down the stairs. She was not prone to hysteria and tantrums, but she got stressed when running behind schedule. Karen refused to own a blow-dryer – it would just frizz up her natural waves, she claimed. I could still see where her long, damp hair had left dark wet spots on the shoulders of her jade-colored linen blouse. Quietly by-passing our guests, she went directly to the kitchen to get the hummus and tabouleh she had prepared earlier. She noisily set the bowls on the dining room table, unintentionally creating a clatter that guaranteed her entrance would not go unnoticed.

I often stared at Karen. She probably took it as endearing while others may have considered it creepy. In truth, I only occasionally stared at her in lust. Usually, I was just wondering why she was still with me, and when she would eventually lose interest. There was no question she could get a better looking man. Like my previous girlfriends, maybe she would make her escape on short notice. There were times that if I'd had the opportunity to escape from myself, I'd have done it.

"Hey Karen, what's up?" Tarini asked, as she followed her into

The Other Face Of Murder

the kitchen. I walked in behind both of them to get some more ice.

"Same old thing. I'm just waking up from a nap. I had the worst migraine today," Karen replied. She massaged the side of her head and her wavy curls bounced along with the movement of her hand.

"Isn't that the worst? I've also been getting tons of headaches lately," said Tarini. As a physician, Tarini couldn't abstain from giving medical advice. Her sincerity, something I've noticed to be common among Hindu women, made her appear so compassionate towards friends and patients. "It's important you get it checked out to make sure it's nothing serious. Did you know women get three times as many headaches as men?" Her right eye twitched involuntarily as she spoke, a tic which I had only recently noticed.

"That doesn't surprise me. It's men that cause them," Karen answered, hoisting herself onto a counter stool. Karen maneuvered like the tomboy she once was, more adept at climbing trees than pirouetting around the room. But this lack of physical gracefulness made her more human in my eyes, since everything else about her seemed perfect. The exceptions included her annoying habit of pressing the snooze alarm six times each morning instead of setting the alarm for an hour later. She also insisted that every location in Portland was only ten minutes away, which resulted in our arriving late to every movie and restaurant reservation.

Grant had followed us into the kitchen. Usually a reliable defender of the male cause, he stopped listening once he spied the Jelly Bellies on the table. Instead, he began devouring them, oblivious to all conversation around him. "These jelly beans are awesome. I mean they could seriously replace fruit."

"You've never had Jelly Bellies before?" Karen inquired, happy for a distracting light topic that would help her forget her headache.

"I've had jelly beans before, but not like these. These are great."

"Well, you sound as if you'd never had one before," Karen went on, "where were you during the Reagan years?" she asked, referring to the famous big jar the president always kept on his desk.

Grant replied defensively, "College, that's where. It's not like I was in Nam or anything, but I've been around. I'll bet most people haven't tried Jelly Bellies." He always said quirky stuff like that. He was a toddler in the Vietnam War years, and nobody would mistake Grant as a war veteran.

Another peculiarity was Grant's tendency to correlate, at random, his own insecurities with the topic at hand. "People often ask me if I'm Asian, but I'm not. My mom drank a lot when she was pregnant with me." That's a classic problem with doctors. They often think every anatomical variation they encounter is a reflection of some disease process. The inferred connection between his mother drinking and him looking Asian baffled Karen, because Grant did not have the kind of slanted eyes that characterize babies with fetal alcohol syndrome. But I had become skilled in following Grant's warped logic.

Back in the living room and over our drinks Earl soon had us in stitches as he related how he had recovered from his typical neurosis of health professionals. Late one night during his second year of med school, he had noticed a nodular three millimeter lesion on his genitals. After scanning every textbook of venereal disease he could find on his crammed bookshelf, he narrowed his self-diagnosis down to one of two rare diseases -- either Lymphogranuloma Venereum or Chancroid. It didn't matter to him that these rarely occurred in North America. Earl convinced himself that he had picked it up from the slutty girlfriend he had during his senior year at Auburn University. Plagued by insomnia, Earl decided that a trip to the Emergency Room was in order. His humiliation deepened when Dr. Jennifer Stover entered the exam room. He hadn't been expecting this. As he undressed with slow hesitation, his timid apology about what he was going to show her only worsened the awkwardness.

Dr. Stover recognized him as a medical student. Not the least bit fazed she took one look at the lesion and, without saying a word, grabbed the nodule between her thumb and index finger and gave a firm squeeze. A small amount of white pus came out of the nodule. Clearly, whatever he had must have been quite serious. He felt the blood drain from his face. Dr. Stover, still silent, took off her gloves and threw them in the trash. She proceeded to wash and dry her hands for another twenty seconds, and opened the door to leave the room. Then she turned and congratulated a red-faced Earl for having the biggest pimple on a penis she had ever seen. She advised him to go home and study the manifestations and treatments of acne.

Inevitably, they still run into each other on hospital shifts. Earl masks his embarrassment by pitching tasteless pick-up lines at her. "You should see me without the pimple."

As a hardened ER doctor, Dr. Stover holds her own with piercing wit. "Earl, without the pimple, there would be nothing there."

I had invited Dr. Stover to our dinner party, but she declined, stating that her ER shift ended at 10 p.m. If she had the energy after work, she would consider stopping by for a late night drink, she said, but it didn't happen. Either she lacked the energy, or Earl genuinely repulsed her. Most likely, it was the latter.

TWO

If there is one thing a medical education has unintentionally taught me, it's that rapid advances in modern medicine generally outpace our ability to reach a consensus on how to deal with the ethical, legal, and natural repercussions. For years I tried to find reasons why I shouldn't accept that lesson as fact. But idealism, in opposition to reality, demanded ignorance and an innocence that is now irretrievably lost.

We have tried reconstructing the details of the event that changed all our lives. None of us remember exactly what was said during our marathon-of-a-dinner, but we had laughed a lot and philosophized a little and told some good stories. We ate and drank well into the night.

Rather than face the diminished visibility of the roads due to Portland's inevitable winter rain, our friends agreed to spend the night. I owned a three-level, five bedroom house, so aside from supplying breakfast, it was no imposition. This wasn't the first time our guests were obliged with overnight hospitality so they could avoid the intimidating combination of vehicles, asphalt, trees, and drink. By the time I made it to our upstairs bedroom, Karen was peacefully asleep. My last memory before collapsing into bed was the majestic view from our bedroom window of Mt. Hood's snow capped peak shining in the light of a pale moon.

The sleep shattering noise that came from downstairs demanded our immediate attention. It left no time to complete a dream which was having a bad ending anyway. Clanging and thuds would not seem unexpected in a house full of inebriated people, yet there was something peculiarly unnerving about that sound. For a second, I wondered if part of an airplane had broken off and hit the house, but then rationalized the improbability of that happening. Karen and I sat bolt upright. Iko, our German Shepherd, was seated at attention in front of our bedroom's closed door, ears cocked, and eyes focused on the knob.

The clock said 4:06 a.m. Had we been asleep a few minutes or a few hours?

"What was that?" Karen whispered. She had the same uneasy look that surfaced a few weeks prior, when I had returned from the hardware store with a how-to book -- *Electrical Wiring Made Easy*.

"I don't know. Probably Earl tripping over something." I figured a quip about the big guy would relieve the tense situation. It didn't. Karen took my remark at face value.

"Earl is sleeping in the basement on the futon. That sound did not come all the way from the basement."

Earlier that night we had all washed away our tensions with liquor. Trying to ignore the consequential headache, I slowly made my way across the bedroom and reluctantly opened the door. One hundred pounds of canine galloped past me, and raced down the stairs. I followed her to the kitchen - unknowingly leaving behind my unseasoned view of life. Sometimes I wonder if that crash was God's way of trying to get my attention.

By the time I got to the kitchen, Iko was barking aggressively in front of the pantry door. She was in a rage, ready to lunge at whatever lurked inside.

I didn't try to quiet her. The dog was not the over-reactive, excitable type. Someone was behind that door. The only time Iko ever acted that crazy was on Tuesday mornings, when she was convinced the garbage men had once again returned to steal our stuff from the driveway. I grabbed a dirty knife that had been left on the cutting board, hoping it would protect me from whatever was hiding in that walk-in pantry. Grant and Earl came up behind me, and fixated on Iko. Earl was clad only in underwear.

"Who's in there?" I yelled.

No answer.

"If anyone is in there you should know that my dog was trained-to-kill in Germany and that we already called the cops."

Grant, and then Earl, grabbed knives from the Wusthof set I had given Karen for her birthday.

Earl noticed that the butcher knife was missing.

"Oh, Jesus..." I whispered. If you want to see what somebody is truly made of, watch what they say and do under pressure. Some, like Abe Lincoln or Washington, were inspired by challenges and displayed genuine greatness. I took a moment to think, and then remarked, "...this unconditionally sucks."

My thoughts momentarily flashed from whether a guy in the pantry had a butcher knife to how I had always wanted a gun, an idea Karen rejected vehemently. How many times had she warned me that every hour in the U.S. four people die from firearms; that having a gun in the home makes it three times more likely that a family member will die from a shooting? I wanted to ask her if she thought the presumed psychopath in the pantry preferred me unarmed, but didn't. In my head I cursed her, and then turned my attention to the problem at hand.

Karen peeked in from the adjacent dining room, and whispered that she thought she had put the butcher knife in the dishwasher. The tone of her voice did not reassure us. The dishwasher was located about two feet from the pantry's doorknob. No one wanted to risk getting that close to the pantry.

Roy made his way into the kitchen. His hands quivered slightly, which was not unusual for him when he was nervous. There was still no sound from the pantry. We hand-signaled each other to retreat to the dining room and formulate a plan. Iko began to snarl and whine, clearly annoyed at my reluctance to take action. Her disapproving demeanor brought to mind a recent encounter with my malcontented, vegetarian neighbor at the annual barbecue block party.

"Should I call the police?" Karen asked me in a barely audible voice.

"Go for it," uttered Roy, but I always loathed involving cops in anything.

"It's four in the morning. We can't be sure there is someone in there. Do we really want to wake the whole neighborhood? It might just be a mouse that knocked over a bunch of soup cans." I knew that wasn't the case. We'd had mice before. Mice wouldn't be strong enough to knock over a single soup can, let alone cause the loud crash we all heard. Iko might have barked once or twice at a mouse. She wouldn't try to tear the door down over one.

Roy spoke up again. "All our cars are in the driveway. Do you think a burglar would really choose to rob a house with that many cars

The Other Face Of Murder

out front?" The hippy geek did make some sense, but none of us paid much attention.

"Where's Tarini?" Karen asked. She was good at asking pertinent questions.

Grant said, "I fell asleep in your basement guest room. I don't think she ever came down to join me. Our car is still out front."

I told the dog to shut up. She quieted down but remained in attack position in front of the pantry door.

"Are you in there, Tarini?" Grant screamed at the door.

No answer. Was Tarini being held hostage behind the door?

Grant walked over, opened the pantry door about 6 inches and backed off. We should all have been feeling terribly hung over, I thought to myself, but a heightened consciousness kindled by fear overcame the lingering intoxication.

Iko saw her cue. She rushed into the pantry, flinging the door open with her strong body, and barked with more frenzy than before. I flipped on the pantry light. There was Tarini immobile on the floor amid cans of refried beans, soup, and a pool of salsa from an adjacent broken jar. I felt her image burn into my retina, and knew it would remain there with the same permanence as a brand on a bull. I rushed to her side. Grant and Earl looked at each other in disbelief, then after a moment of startled hesitation, joined me at her side. There were no cuts on her. No signs of trauma, but she wasn't breathing.

THREE

The events that followed are almost picture perfect in my memory. Grant freaked out because he couldn't feel a pulse. I started chest compressions. He gave rescue breaths. Karen called the 911 dispatcher.

Tarini didn't feel cold, but she didn't feel warm either. Her petite body was naked under a long white shirt. Her lips were blue, and her hands and feet appeared mottled. The pupils of her once beautiful emerald green eyes were dilated and fixed. If the eyes are the windows to the soul, as some say, then her soul seemed to have departed. When the brain isn't getting oxygen, it starts dying after four minutes. We had wasted precious time being idiots outside the pantry door. Was she not breathing that entire time? As a critical-care physician, I knew the grim statistics for surviving an out-of-hospital cardiac arrest, but the thought of not generating a successful resuscitation didn't cross my mind, nor apparently the minds of any of my friends.

The world seemed to me to be divided primarily into two groups of people. Those who credit a puppet-master in the sky for pulling all the strings, and those who believe we're on our own. Then there are confused folks like me who are on both sides of the aisle theologically. I wasn't naïve enough to think Tarini's heart would start on its own by divine intervention, but if God wanted to assist in the matter, I was all for the help.

None of it felt real. We had participated in plenty of CODE BLUE cardiac arrests, but always in the hospital where the environment was controllable, and personnel back-up, drugs, and defibrillators were plentiful. Usually there was a degree of separation between the doctors and the patients that allowed for clear and logical thinking. Our personal feelings about Tarini bred an intensely intimate and visceral response. Panic never helps a resuscitation effort, and we were all panicked. People watch heroic CPR on television where the victim wakes up with Pamela Anderson or another Baywatch beauty pressed against his lips, and assume it always works that way in real life. But, this wasn't television. There were no dramatized characters saying, "Come on man, you've got to make it. Don't you die on me now!"

We were all trying to stay focused on getting the job done for Tarini. Consistent with the statistics, we were not reviving her despite our best efforts. In the background, Karen was screaming at the 911 operator to get help to us faster. We momentarily gained composure and then got back into sequence. Perspiration born from raw exasperation dripped out of every skin pore. Every few minutes or so, I felt another one of Tarini's ribs fracture during my chest compressions, as is the usual case in prolonged CPR. Whether or not Tarini felt anything was impossible to discern. She wasn't displaying any signs of suffering. A grimace or a moan would have been gratifying in a situation so desperate.

Patients who have pulled out of a close brush with death have told me that the dying process paradoxically made them feel more alive than ever before. Not only on a psychological level of being able to understand completely what's important and what they will miss, but on a physical level as well. They cherish each palpitation of blood in their vessels. Each breath becomes so monumental that they can't imagine how most days proceeded without them ever thinking about breathing.

We only die once, and each experience is intimate and unique. Death is something we don't usually schedule into our lives, but the disease of mortality is an affliction we all encounter, eventually. As a frequent observer of the process, it's something I've thought a lot about, but that experience complicated everything.

When performing CPR, it's essential to allow for a brief pause in chest compressions to feel for a pulse every couple of minutes. If the heart starts beating you don't want to continue traumatizing the chest. My fingers pressed into Tarini's neck in an attempt to detect blood flow in her carotid artery. For a second I thought there was a pulse, but then realized my panic had caused an amateurish error. My own pulse was pounding so hard in my fingertips that I had attributed it to Tarini's heart. When I palpated my own carotid artery with my other hand, the pulses in both hands were unambiguously synchronous with each other.

The paramedics finally arrived. They hooked up the heart monitor, and we scrutinized the dreadful flat rhythm of asystole. Tarini's heart did not contain even a slight trace of electricity to shock it back to life. I mustered up the courage to look at Grant. He stood silently, staring at the monitor. I fixated on his small chin scar that he once claimed was from a tumble in kindergarten due to an untied shoelace. Then he turned his head downward, buried his chin in his chest, and began to sob convulsively.

FOUR

In the hours succeeding her death, we had experienced a handful of clinically recognized stages of grief that generally follow the death of a loved one. First was denial. Nothing made sense. Tarini was only thirty-six and appeared to have no underlying medical problems. Women her age just don't spontaneously have cardiac arrest. What on earth was she doing in the pantry anyway? Late night munchies are powerful, not deadly. Next came the anger and guilt. Why had we been so stupid and weak? If we hadn't been fearful of opening the door, we could have saved her. Courage is doing what you're afraid to do. None of us displayed courage that night, and it wrecked our egos. The final stage of dealing with grief is acceptance, which transpires when you realize that nothing can change what has already occurred. Without acceptance, inner peace becomes impossible. Meaningless hurting is harder to accept than calamity with a reason.

You don't have to be a genius to suspect foul play when a young woman is found in nothing but a night shirt, alone, and dead at four in the morning. It was exceedingly unlikely she died of alcohol toxicity if she was able to get up and walk to the pantry. Someone who died of alcohol poisoning would have been unconscious for a long time prior to death.

At the scene of her death, Earl and I had made educated guesses as to what happened. Perhaps it was a burst aneurysm, massive seizure, or a major embolism to her lungs. None of the guesses made medical sense to me. There was no question this death required an autopsy. Without it, we couldn't rule out homicide.

I called the coroner's office the next day.

"This is Doctor Weissman. You received a body yesterday by the name of Tar…"

"I'm sorry Doctor; we haven't received any bodies in the last 48 hours."

"No bodies? Are you sure about that?"

"Yes, Doctor. Aside from the coroner, there are only two other employees here, and the other one is on vacation. I assure you I would have known if we received any recent admissions."

"Thank you very much for your time."

"Thank you, Doctor."

I was only a little shocked to hear that. In former times, if there were even a slight suspicion of homicide or suicide; the case would go straight to the coroner. Nowadays, there needs to be a very strong suspicion of foul play before anyone can spend the meager resources awarded to the coroner's office. Since there was no motive, no trauma, and the medical technicians had witnessed prominent physicians trying to save Tarini, the police believed her death was due to natural causes.

There are three groups of people that taxpayers and city councilmen won't spend money on -- the homeless, the mentally ill, and the already-dead. Ironically, taxpayers are willing to pay for workout equipment in prisons, but the county coroners who deal with the victims of crimes committed by brawny ex-prisoners have few resources. I drove to my office at Good Samaritan hospital. There, the medical records computer revealed Tarini's recent admission to the pathology morgue. At least the emergency room doctor was smart enough to realize that, at a minimum, Tarini deserved an autopsy, even if it wasn't a case for the coroner. The post-mortem had been assigned to one of our better pathologists, Dr. Klaus Vanwaggen. He was a bizarre character, even for a pathologist. Impressive skill and knowledge did not make up for the fact that Klaus was one of the most annoying men born in the last hundred years.

Your medical specialty tends to say a lot about the type of person you are. Studies show that most psychiatrists go into the field because they are trying to figure out their own particular neuroses. Why pathologists choose their field has always remained a mystery to me. If you don't like talking to patients, why not pick the more lucrative field of radiology? Pathologists deal all day long with either surgically removed tissue or dead people. They are some of the smartest doctors out there, and almost always make the correct diagnosis. They just make it too late, from the patients' perspective.

Every pathology department I've been in is located in the hospital's basement. Patient areas of a hospital continuously get refurbished and modernized, but the pathology department with its pervasive smell of formaldehyde remains unchanged from the day the hospital was built until its demolition.

Finding your way around a large hospital is tough, but navigating the basement is an art. Endless halls of cold concrete floors, gray painted walls without landmarks, and unfinished ceilings with pipes going in all directions almost guarantee at least one wrong turn. However, on that morning, I arrived at Dr. Vanwaggen's office as if guided by an internal compass. I never knock because he would never consider answering. I just walked in.

Klaus Vanwaggen was a tall, obese man with a scraggy Santa Claus beard and peculiar mannerisms. Almost monthly I would visit him to discuss a challenging case. He would review pathology slides with me in a technical language I could barely understand despite my extensive training. His thick German accent always made it all the more toilsome.

As usual, he did not look up from his microscope despite hearing me enter.

"Klaus, you've got to give me information on this one."

"Dr. Jerry Vize-man, she iss not your patient. Her medical information iss only privilege to her doctor and family."

"I've never been more serious about any case in my life Klaus. You've got to tell me, and show me, everything you find."

"Are you vorried about zomezing zpezifically, Dr. Vize-man?"

"You know as well as I that thirty-six year-old marathon runners do not wind up dead in the pathology morgue every day."

"Dr. Vize-man, you only zee deaths you have personal involvement in az a pheezyician. Vee zee every death in zee hospital. Zeveral times a year vee do zee young healtzy people zpontaneouzly die, my friend. Vuntz in a vhile tragedy ztrikez. A brain aneureezem, a heart attack, you never know my friend. Teeze tingz happen."

That was the world Klaus lived in. A world of body parts and stiff cadavers. A world of logic and indifference. Was Klaus right? Maybe I was trying to find too much meaning, where meaning wasn't meant to be found. I was a doctor, not a novelist. Fiction writers, often placing false significance on tragic events, fall into the trap of giving illness and death deeper meaning. In literature, a bulimic character's purging always implies a need to get some sort of memory out of her system. The truth is bulimics usually just want to be thin. The purging doesn't signify anything other than that. Still, when it came to Tarini, there had to be underlying purpose and intentions that hadn't yet surfaced.

"But it wasn't an aneurysm or heart attack, was it?" It was more of a statement than a question.

"No! It vazz not," he forcefully replied. He had not once looked up from his microscope.

It is not easy to intimidate a large German man. I got two inches from his ear and spoke loudly. "Klaus, you will tell me everything you know about this one. Everything. You got that?"

He turned to look at me. There was a large yellow sleep crust in the corner of his left eye that he hadn't bothered to remove. I didn't flinch even though I wanted to back off. Our noses we're almost touching. His eye booger wasn't bothering me, but his breath was stunning my olfactory system. He was one of those guys, who after he used a phone, the next person to use that phone would still smell his breath on the plastic.

"Dr. Vize-man, and v-when I need zee favor?"

The aroma accompanying his question irritated the membranes lining my nostrils. Did he gorge on sauerkraut flavored cereal for breakfast that morning?

"Anything anytime. Anything."

Damn. A dangerous deal had just been made with the fire-breathing devil.

"Come back tomorrow afternoon pleaze."

"I'll be here at 8 a.m., Klaus."

FIVE

I stopped by Earl's house to see if he had any original thoughts pertaining to Tarini. It was an unusual Portland day, sunny and without rain. Earl was slumped on his porch swing having a bottle of McTarnahans Ale. A menthol toothpick dangled from his mouth. I sat down on the black iron bench a short distance from the swing and noticed the spectacular red rose bushes blooming on his lawn. They glistened as if they had been dipped in wax. Roses are a symbol of love and death, but I couldn't solely blame the roses for eliciting my sentiments connected to Tarini. Everything was reminding me of her. Anytime I saw an Indian woman, or the hospital, or a female doctor, or a blue car like the one she drove, it awakened memories. I was obsessed, and removing her from my mind was impossible.

"As an oncologist I deal with death daily. I've got to admit I'm taking this one pretty darn hard," Earl stated. He handed me a bottle of ale that I swiftly gulped in an attempt to lubricate my chafed nerves.

"Earl, your patients are your patients. Tarini was your *friend*. Of course, this is going to be harder. None of us will ever get over this completely," I responded.

"Jerry, in my specialty my patients become my friends. Their feathers are ruffled, but they look towards me as the rock, the foundation from which the fight of their life will be waged. Sometimes with only a snowball's chance in hell, they push on. In your specialty, you don't have as much time to bond with your dying patients. Already close to death, they get fast tracked into your critical care unit at any time of the day or night. Then you stick a tube down their throat and put them on ventilators. They couldn't talk to you, even if they wanted to communicate. My patients, on the other hand, consult me the second their cancer is diagnosed. The battle against their diseases can go on for years. Faith is the most powerful emotion after love and hate. My patients put their faith in me as if I'm kinfolk. They believe I will do everything in my power to reverse the curse that plans to rob their future. I become their most trusted ally and that makes me their *friend and doctor*." As if to reassure himself, he declared, "I'm devastated about Tarini, but we all must go on. Wounds eventually heal."

"You don't think there is anything strange about the way she died? I mean, come on Earl. Stuff like that just doesn't happen everyday," I said.

"Jerry, what are you suggesting? We are all great friends. No one would hurt that girl, let alone kill her. This whole thing is horrible, but whatever happened was not anyone's fault. I'll bet a thousand dollars the autopsy provides a logical explanation for her death. When we have that explanation, we still won't get closure. More intelligence won't beget approval and understanding. A beast in the slaughter line doesn't care about explanations for us wanting to harvest a filet mignon from its carcass."

"So tell me, how did you know she is having an autopsy?" I asked Earl. He was slightly taken aback at my inquiry. My voice had begun to sound a bit like some Hollywood detective.

Earl justified himself. "Who wouldn't do an autopsy in this situation? When someone this young dies, you need to find the cause of death. Just because an autopsy needs to be done, does not mean there was a murder, Jerry. You're focusing too much on the 'why' of all this. Grieving is important. Shed as many tears as you need to. But don't ever question me or any of your friends in a tone of accusation."

While Earl at times was arrogant, he was a genuinely good guy at heart. His conscience can be well hidden, but does exist, like the chirping insects you never see on a summer night. I only observed vehement mean-spiritedness once, after he had a nasty disagreement with the hospital Chief Financial Officer over the budget and floor plan for the new chemotherapy center.

The vengeful idea came to him after seeing those advertisements in the weekend newspaper for decorative collector plates, the ones that say:

> For a limited time only!
> Own this special limited edition SNOW TIGER plate.
> Hand signed by the artist.
> We bill you four easy payments of just $9.99 each.

For six weeks in a row he had various series of plates sent and billed to that unfortunate administrator's house. Earl never has shown remorse for the huge hassles that must have created for our CFO. When asked about it, he defends himself as if the matter were justified. "The guy was a jerk! Besides, I did him a favor. The Dale Earnhardt commemorative plate is already selling on eBay for more than a hundred dollars."

Another singular trait of Earl's was that, for a smart guy, he was always trying to seem a lot smarter. The first time he invited me to his house, he tried to dupe me into thinking he was a genius. After getting us some beer, he turned on the television. Jeopardy was on. Earl proceeded to answer every question before the contestants even rang in. I had aced honors classes throughout my schooling, and met some brilliant people, but had never witnessed such a broad array of knowledge. He would have convinced me, except that during a commercial break, I noticed a small amount of static fuzz at the bottom of the screen. A glance at the VCR showed it was in the PLAY mode.

Instead of looking me in the eye, Earl gazed above my head as if he had a vision that only he could see. "I'm not mad at you Jerry. You just have to realize we are all hurting too. Everybody cared about Tarini. This is not only about you."

"I'm sorry, Earl. I really am. You know I trust you completely. I'm just going to have to work my unsettled feelings out on this one," I said.

"That's fine. Let me share with you one of my favorite sayings. *A man wearing a watch knows what time it is, but if you wear two watches you'll never be sure what time it is.* The point being, don't make things more complicated than they already are. There is a lot on all our plates right now. No point in going for seconds. Allow yourself to grieve, but don't focus on your grief when worthier thoughts are trying to enter your conscious. Constantly thinking about a tragedy keeps a person in a state of hyper-arousal. It won't let you focus on life. Instead, it centers your life around pain, to the exclusion of pleasure."

Earl seemed to have a point. His career as an oncologist had provided for plenty of opportunity to devise rationales for overcoming calamity. While there may have been differences between us, I was feeling inadequate about my coping. One would think I'd be more accepting of mortality after many years on the job. For understandable reasons, Tarini's death naturally provoked new feelings.

    While sitting with Earl, I let my thoughts shift briefly to the recent news photos of long lines of people desperate to donate blood following the September 11th World Trade Center aftermath. The twin towers were modern marvels that took such effort to build, and were destroyed in a single day by a madman living in a cave in Afghanistan. Our fear of terrorism had driven us toward irrationality, and we applauded our irrational behavior. From a medical perspective, I knew that much of the blood wouldn't be needed, that it would soon expire and need to be disposed of. Psychologically, though, the people in those donation lines needed to feel they were part of the solution, even if their efforts were futile. Were my efforts similarly irrational and futile? Maybe my goose chase to find an answer was in reality a diversion to postpone the inevitable mourning process. Father used to tell me that, *sometimes the biggest false step is not taking one at all.* It was great advice, even though I now know that much of the advice he gave me was reaped from fortune cookies. I just didn't want to make any irrational mistakes and ignore the momentous tragedy that had transpired in my house.

SIX

Memory furnishes illusions which our minds can use for ill, or to advantage. Dwelling on the memory of the dinner party we gave on the night Tarini died became a neurotic obsession. We had been sitting around my dining table, bowls loaded up with the spinach, apple, and Gorgonzola salad that Karen had tossed together. I grabbed the opportunity to speak while everyone else chewed.

"So here's how my day started. At dawn I was in the ICU tending a cancer patient fighting a raging bacterial infection that had put her body in shock." Shock, as my colleagues understood, means that the cardiovascular system had started to collapse. "After doing everything I could medically do for this patient, I soon realized the situation had become irreversibly fatal. The two other physicians on the case agreed the prognosis was hopeless."

With a full mouth of spinach, Grant blurted, "Same story, different day." And there was truth to that. Death occurs in every hospital every day.

With the exception of Karen and Roy, we were all physicians, and among the most competent and dedicated in Portland. We were professionals who took our jobs and patients' concerns seriously. Our ability to unwind and act immature after work should not be misinterpreted. Time and experience can wear down some professional folks with strenuous occupations. Mandatory fun when away from our vocations was a doctrine we abided by to repel burnout. We were in our late-thirties, in the prime of our careers, and there was nothing jaded about any of us yet.

Karen constantly reminded me how boring medical conversations were for those who couldn't follow the terminology and complexities of the ailment being discussed. Seeking a compromise, I tried to illuminate with a human interest version that non-medical folks at the dinner table might appreciate.

"Yes, different day, same story," I continued, "but it was

unusually hard to communicate with this patient's daughter whose mother was in the dying process. The culture of modern American medicine is to prolong life. Physicians want to advocate for their patients' best interests, and usually that means advocating for keeping people alive as well as keeping hope alive. It's not like I'm for euthanasia or similar insanities. But, allowing death to forge ahead when there is no stopping it is perhaps something worth getting comfortable with."

Oregon became the first state in our nation to legalize physician assisted suicide in 1997. I had remained an outspoken critic. My father had committed suicide, and I knew that no family could fully recover from the consuming anger and grief that such an action leaves behind. From my point of view, the idea that a licensed professional healer entrusted with saving lives would knowingly kill people was preposterous and morally wrong. Accepting the natural deaths of my patients was hard enough. Speeding up the process of dying nauseated me.

While it is a beautiful state with terrific people, the laws in Oregon sometimes appear to be drafted by lunatics. It's illegal to pump your own gas in Oregon. Adults in Oregon are prohibited from showing a minor any piece of classical artwork which depicts sexual excitement. Other state laws include the rule that no more than two people may share a single beverage, and all pets must be restrained in cars with specially designed pet seatbelts. However, if you want your doctor to kill you – that's no problem at all.

"Well, not everyone is easy to talk to. The more people don't want to hear you, then the smarter your argument may be," said Grant, still chewing. "One of my heroes has always been Charles Darwin. His discovery refuted most contentions that humans have a special place above nature. While humans are sometimes able to live outside the usual laws of nature through the use of technology, our place within the universe is no more special than that of an ape or a spider."

Earl was not impressed. "Brilliant, Grant. Please share with us some more of your senior year thesis."

"Listen, this directly relates to Jerry's morning," said Grant. "By showing how evolution worked, Darwin taught us that who we are psychologically and socially cannot be understood until we understand who we are biologically. All living creatures are composed of cells that have a finite existence. Family members will often refuse to address the biological realities of terminal illness and focus only on the social and psychological side. This is unfortunate. Conversely, some doctors forget about the social and psychological aspects of an illness and focus only on its biological aspects. This is also unfortunate. It is imperative that patients, families, and doctors attempt a biopsychosocial approach to serious illness. Darwin used reason against the false beliefs of the masses. Creationists still hold misdirected convictions against evolution and the connection all life on Earth shares. I am not one to argue against faith. On the other hand, when faith is used to argue against reason and reality, the result is ignorance and denial, which was the issue with the daughter of Jerry's patient."

Earl started laughing and mocking Grant. "I love it man! Someone call PBS so we can do a special on this."

Roy looked at Earl as though he were a barbaric caveman. He was sensitive to people making fun of others, even if Grant was thick-skinned. Roy didn't speak up though; in fact, he had been particularly quiet during the meal. That skinny guy seemed ravenous and was eating like a woman pregnant with triplets. Knowing Roy, I didn't hold the food responsible for his silence.

Roy was shy when it came to conversing with more than one person. I first met him at a coffee shop soon after moving to The Rose City. Noticing that I held a copy of *The Time Machine* by H.G. Wells, he asked if I believed in time travel. I expressed the opinion that the divisions of time could be different in other parts of the universe; so time travel would certainly be a possibility, if one could somehow tap into an alternative time continuum. That impressed him, and before we knew it we were discussing everything from proper coffee bean cultivation to why Geisha women paint their faces porcelain white. He revealed a preoccupation with science fiction, especially for writers such as Gene Roddenberry of Star Trek fame, who had created future utopias where money doesn't exist, nobody starves, and diversity is celebrated.

Tarini suddenly interrupted my musing to defend her man. "I think Grant has some brilliant points. Friends often ask me what is the worst thing I've ever seen in the hospital, expecting to hear, perhaps, about some gruesome trauma case. We've all seen plenty of that stuff. Still, the worst thing a doctor sees are the faces of family members when you tell them a loved one has died or will die. The daughter of Jerry's ICU patient was distressed. Everyone deals with grief differently. She couldn't accept the biological reality of a dying body. There is no typical reaction to the death of a loved one."

Tarini then repeated softly, "There is no typical reaction to the death of a loved one."

Karen, who had been quiet, spoke up. "The question really becomes, when has a person died? It seems to be more a philosophical question than a medical question these days. If you can't talk, eat, or communicate, and need a machine to act as your heart and lungs, it's still not considered death in the United States. People can hang out on life support for literally decades."

Earl admonished everyone. "Why don't we let Jerry here finish his story? We don't even know what the reaction of the daughter ultimately was. At this point we're making arguments that are a few French fries short of a happy meal."

I began where I had left off, before everyone had chipped in. "So I told this daughter, 'your mother is very sick. I don't think any of the medicines we are giving her are going to reverse the situation. I think it would be reasonable to focus our efforts on making your mother comfortable. At this point we are probably prolonging her death, but not her life. It is my experience in these situations that a year or two from now the family won't remember whether their loved one died on a Friday or a Tuesday. You will remember only how the final days went, and you will feel better if you can rationalize that at least your mother was comfortable in the last days of her life.' To which the daughter replied, '*All right, Doc. But what I'm sayin' is let's not beat around the bush. O.K. You know what I'm sayin'? If my momma is sick, I want to know how sick she is. Because I can handle it.*' And, I told her again. 'Um, well. What I'm trying to say is I do think your mother is extremely sick and that she is dying.' This daughter then looks at me and asks, '*So what are you suggesting, Doc?*' There just wasn't any getting through to her."

With annoyance Karen asked, "Are you using Ebonics talk to degrade this poor woman?"

"Hell no, that's exactly how she talked. I'm just giving an

accurate picture of what was happening. This just happened to be an African-American woman whose upper arms were so big they hung over her elbows, and who clearly didn't have much education beyond reading the paper tray liners at fast food joints. Listen, I've had articulate white patients who were even more clueless and in denial about the dying process, but this is who I happened to be dealing with today. Anyway, I said to this woman, 'We could consider trying to keep her more comfortable and not focus as much on therapeutics.' And then she asks me, '*so that is gonna help her heart?*' I told her, 'No. I don't think anything we are doing is going to help her heart. The damage is irreversible at this stage.' I spelled it out it in the most convincing manner I could."

Tarini explained, "She just wasn't ready to hear all that." Her hand twitched a bit as she spoke and she accidentally dropped her fork. For someone with a lot of manners and class, it seemed so uncharacteristic.

Earl diverted our attention. "Well, who the hell *is* ready to hear all that? Jerry still has to give the family the information. Like it or not, that daughter needs to make decisions in such a circumstance. The cat will remain calm and dignified until the big mean doggy enters the room. This daughter was facing down a big mean doggie in trying to come to terms with end-stage illness."

"Absolutely right, Earl." I was happy to get the support. "But, she wasn't going to make any decisions no matter what. That was the frustrating element. Instead, the daughter became bothered and said, '*It sounds to me like she need a heart specialist.*' Happy to respond to that statement, I said, 'Your mother has been seen by a heart specialist and that's his opinion as well.' But, she just ignored all that and asked, '*So what do we do now?*' The conversation had become hopeless. Was it denial? Was it lack of education? Was I not communicating clearly? 'We keep fighting and doing what we're doing and pray she gets better,' I finally told her."

I had presumed that by bringing the case up at dinner, I would get other opinions. I had felt conflicted about taking away the daughter's hope. On rare occasion I have seen miracles and been proven wrong. Doctors are burdened by the decision of whether to offer hope, which may be deceitful, or to be painfully honest. Adding pessimism to already despondent situations always evokes an ugly practical concern. Even if we could extend the patient's life by a week or a month, is it worth the enormous resources of time, emotion, and money it would take for heroic gestures?

As was our custom, Karen and I had encouraged our guests to take a long, relaxing break between the salad and entree. We poured more drinks and the party continued.

Karen, after getting some nutrition, said her headache was gone. "Come on Karen; tell them about your awful adventure in Wyoming," I pleaded, hoping it would relieve the morbid atmosphere of the discussion.

"They don't want to hear about that," she answered.

"Yes we do!" everyone said in unison. Karen took a sip of wine and began. "Well, several weeks ago I took a snowmobile tour with some old high school friends at Yosemite. The park was beautiful and the ride exciting, but suddenly out of nowhere a dog came running beside my snowmobile. He seemed to be playful, but I was afraid he'd jump in front of my 800-pound noise-polluter and get hurt, so I slowed down. The dog jumped on my lap, and through my snow-pants and long underwear, bit into my thigh. Maybe he was punishing me for the noise and pollution."

"You're kidding me?" asked Grant.

"Nope. When the park service came, the chase scene actually got pretty funny. The rangers' comments over their CBs sounded like a cartoon. 'Suspect is in sight and moving quickly on all fours.' Or, 'We got him in sight and we're right on his tail.' They never were able to catch the furry perpetrator. This was unfortunate because it meant my having to experience the full rabies vaccination series."

Tarini interjected with, "Oh, no. That's painful. That being said, it's a blessing to have an easy fix like vaccines in a situation like that."

That's the irony of modern medicine. Easy fixes and successful outcomes for a myriad of conditions. Yet, in a matter of hours, a young Tarini - although surrounded by doctors - encountered a diametrically opposite fate.

SEVEN

Two days after Tarini's death, I went to visit Roy. Of all my friends, Roy was the most fragile, least stable, and above all, the least likely murder suspect. Besides, since my visit with Earl, I no longer was in the 'everyone is a suspect' frame of mind.

I drove to the southwest division of the city, to a tree-lined block of houses where Roy was renting a moderate sized tranquil bungalow. From the driveway, I observed him slowly pacing back and forth across the living room, his hands buried deep in his pant pockets and his shoulders hunched up. The door was open. He paced towards me as I walked in.

"Have you found out what happened to Tarini?" he asked.

"Not yet. She's getting an autopsy."

He stopped pacing and started tapping his right foot up and down as if there was a bug underneath his shoe that just wouldn't die. "Oh man, that's terrible. Really terrible."

Roy noticed me looking at his foot. He stopped tapping and started jingling change in his pocket.

I tried to reassure him. "We'll find out soon what exactly happened."

"Oh, good. That's really good." He sat down on a creaking maple rocking chair that he had imperfectly refinished himself, and began rocking.

Roy's father had owned a small antique shop where Roy learned to love handcrafted furniture and to shun anything factory-made. When his father died, he inherited all the furniture, but instead of selling it, he brought it all home – every item in the store. He cherished the furniture even beyond his father's ashes because the furniture was a more tangible reminder of the person his dad had been. Still, Roy wasn't about to relinquish his own belongings, just to create a magazine-perfect layout. So, on top of a beautifully carved cherry wood side table sat an orange day-glow lava lamp. Above his 100 year-old Victorian hand-carved walnut sleigh bed hung a chrome-framed, original Star Wars poster. Like Roy himself, the total effect was incongruous. However, losing a father while still being at an important developmental stage was something I knew about all too well. We shared that in common, but almost never discussed it openly.

Roy reached across an elegant nineteenth century pine coffee table and offered me M&Ms from a hand-blown contemporary glass bowl made by a popular local artisan. I watched as he rocked back and forth, devouring M&Ms. When he got to the last one, he lifted it to eye level and solemnly addressed it. "You are the last survivor," he declared, as he plopped it on his tongue. "The force is strong with this one."

In addition to losing our fathers, a legacy of mental illness in the family was also something we had in common. Roy's mother was battling with schizophrenia, and my father had been a manic-depressive. Worried about developing psychosis like his mother, Roy feared his inner demons. He struggled to stay unstressed, and fought any influence that he thought would unbalance him. I, on the other hand, dealt with that albatross by occupying myself with the pursuit of numerous academic undertakings. Diverting my subconscious with anything, even constant test taking, was better than solitude. That obsessiveness manifested itself in achievements that I hadn't originally intended, such as getting a medical degree at the age of twenty-four. Unlike me, Roy seemed to lack ambition and direction. He planned his future one day at a time, without maximizing his highly marketable skills. Employment in a corporate environment where the purpose of business is to increase earnings, and where the pressure of making huge profits often trumps ethics, would probably have driven him into the abyss of insanity.

Despite his wavering constitution, pure evil would need to threaten the universe itself before Roy turned homicidal. While nobody lives free of all sin, there surely was nothing about Tarini that would have motivated someone like Roy to murder.

Roy's conscience required simple, logical, and fair answers. That's why he read science fiction instead of newspapers. Justice and equality existed in comics. The real world was where the strong exploited the weak, poor, and vulnerable, and so often got away with it.

Albert Einstein once said, *'Imagination is more important than knowledge'*. So maybe Roy did have his priorities straight.

Friends wondered if Roy's sci-fi infatuated mind was a blessing or a curse. It did seem more creative than immersing oneself in televised sports and drinking. Instead of following the NFL, he dreamed up utopian scenarios in which he rescued Princess Leia, married her, and settled on Endor among the Ewoks. Sometimes things got a little weird such as the time he nicknamed his pecker Darth. However, it was all harmless, and even entertaining. Fortunately for him, Roy combined his highly developed imagination with amazing technological skill, which served him well as a freelance software programmer. He fortuitously landed in the right city, for Portland had come a long way from its past economic dependence on otter-pelt trading and logging. Now the majority of jobs are in the service and computer industry.

Figuring I'd relax and stay a while, I reached for a comfortable floor pillow. A thick Japanese anime book slid off the top of the cushion onto the carpet. The title of the elaborately illustrated text was "Princess Mononoke".

"That comic book has got to exceed three hundred pages," I remarked.

"It's not a comic. That is flawlessly hand drawn animation in combination with stunning computer-generated images. True art, my friend."

"Well, I just don't see how one's interest can be maintained by an *animation* book that is that long," I responded.

"Yeah. First of all it's not just a book. It's an opus. Second, *Princess Mononoke* was originally a movie." Roy, fervently wrapped up in the merit of the book, pointed at it with affection. "This here masterpiece is a collectible that showcases the brilliance of master director Hiyao Miyazaki. This ain't Disney. This is a gazillion times more innovative and thought-provoking than The Lion King."

"So, you're reading about the animation in a movie you already saw?"

"Yes, and it's my third time reading it too." Roy got up and walked over to the fridge. "Do you want a drink?"

"Sure, water will do." He handed me a warm can of carbonated water. "Is the fridge working, Roy?"

He replied, "The damn droid became in-operational last week."

I changed the subject. "How's your mother doing?"

"She is back in the hospital. She didn't take her meds for a couple days. I've been notably lax in visiting her this past week. Without human interaction she loses her grip on reality quickly."

Roy's mother had been an heiress whose family made a fortune in the mining business. Never good at holding onto money, she lost the last of her inheritance when she donated the remainder of her fortune to the 1992 Ross Perot presidential campaign. She had delusions about Perot's big ears being radar antennas that picked up messages from aliens throughout the universe. If he had won the presidency, he would have been able to unite the entire universe, she believed. That must have been quite a day for the Perot campaign telemarketer who had randomly called Roy's mother for a contribution.

"Maybe you should get her a pet. It would focus her and give her a responsibility," I suggested. Too often, I gave Roy unsolicited advice regarding his mother. Nothing qualified me as an expert on dealing with schizophrenia. Keeping my mouth shut would have been in everybody's best interest. Whatever I might have done better regarding the dysfunctional relationship I had with my father, it had no bearing on Roy's relationship with his dysfunctional mother. Besides, advice on how to handle somebody else's family member should only be given if requested, and maybe not even then.

"Tried that. I adopted a mutt from the pound. She loved Spock, but she was too sick to have that kind of responsibility. I had to give the dog back to the pound."

"Why? Did she neglect it?"

"Very much the opposite. She couldn't get her possessed mind off Spock. Maybe I should have started with a hamster or something. A dog was too big of a step. The first day she got Spock, she rushed him to the veterinarian. She told me she was worried about some red thing that kept sticking out of him."

"She took him to the vet because of erections?"

"Yep, and it only got worse from there," Roy said. "By the way, how is Grant holding up?"

I replied, "I plan to go over and see him soon. Karen visited him this morning, but I haven't spoken with her since breakfast. You want to come with me to Grant's house tomorrow?"

"I don't know, man. I kind of had it out with him at your dinner party. I feel bad about cutting on his Republican beliefs and all."

"I doubt he even slightly cares about that. Besides, that's how you feel about Republicans."

"Yeah, but it's not how I feel about Grant. He's a cool guy. He isn't one of those dudes who only cares about himself and his money."

"They've got a name for that. He's a compassionate conservative."

"Compassionate conservative? Oh yeah, someone once explained that those are the guys who step over the homeless instead of stepping on them."

"Kind of like that," I chuckled. "Anyway, you two have always had these disagreements and you're still friends. Nothing is changed today."

"True. I'm just tired of fighting with Grant. Even after you went to bed we were still going at it for a while."

"You and Grant were still arguing?"

"Yeah. All about the same stuff. He's just been crimping my style man. Such a drag because it was rubbing off on Tarini. The longer she was with Grant, the less tenderhearted towards the human race she became. It's as if she were drifting towards the dark side like Anakin Skywalker."

"I never knew you felt that way."

"Yeah. Unfortunately, her death may be the thing that brings Grant and me closer on the things that are important. I think the arguments will cool down. Anyway, I'm just emotional now, and probably giving him a bum rap. In reality, we are all just as responsible as Grant for Tarini's demise."

Clearly, he too, felt blameworthy about not promptly opening the pantry door.

I remembered listening to their stupid disagreements at the dinner party. Grant had been in one of his moods before the meal. Nobody thought much about it at the time. His bickering actually started with Earl, before he moved on to Roy. Tarini and Karen had miscalculated how long they'd need to stir the delicate lobster and scallop risotto, which resulted in the men having too much time to tend to their drinks.

Grant, as always when he got his buzz on, changed the subject to sex.

"So Earl, would you ever sleep with a hooker?"

"Not knowingly I sure wouldn't."

"What the hell does that mean?"

"That means I have slept with a hooker, but I didn't know it at the time."

"So you're saying you got a freebie?"

"Sort of like that."

"Oh Jesus! Please stop beating around the bush. I have to know what happened."

Earl explained, "Well I've slept with a hooker many times. It's just that she wasn't a hooker when I met her fine self. I dated her in high school for almost a year. I'll tell you this girl was as limber as a dish rag. A few years ago I was surfing porn on the net and I came across a picture that looked just like her. But, I dismissed it lickety split. There was just no way it could be her I told myself."

"How did you find out it was her?"

"Last year e-mails started arriving from various friends. She works at that there Bunny Ranch in Nevada. It was featured on an HBO special and some people recognized her on the show. That place is a big bucks whorehouse, I tell ya. It costs $1,000 per hour to be with a girl there."

"That is big money."

"Yep, I reckon I got about $200,000 in free service during my high school days. It was as if the girl had WD-40 on the zipper of her jeans."

Grant pried no further. Standing up to make his way to the refrigerator for a refill he turned to Roy, and said, "I called you yesterday, but you weren't home."

"Yeah, I was out smacking around whitey."

"Smacking around whitey?"

"Yeah, you know golfing."

"You know Roy, you're the only hippy I know who golfs."

"Why would you think hippies don't golf?"

"I just thought you all spent your days sitting around depressed, smoking pot and listening to Pink Floyd." Grant said, with a smile on his face. "Floyd fans are simply the most miserable people in the world. For your own mental well-being I suggest you stop listening to that crap."

"We hippies have normal lives despite our alternative takes on reality. And by the way, Pink Floyd is mind expanding and not depressing," Roy responded.

"Pink Floyd is depressing," said Grant.

"Whatever, Grant. Your straight and narrow ass is the last person who should be talking to others about mental well-being. I mean, Jiminy Creepers; you're a fucking Republican. Conserve! Conserve! That's what you conservatives want to do. If you guys want to conserve, why don't you start conserving the environment, dude?"

Grant took it with a grin. He imagined Roy visiting left wing chat rooms late at night to berate the economic, political, and environmental legacies of the Bush presidencies.

"I'm for conserving tax breaks for the rich," Grant said. "But my social opinions are liberal on most issues; like gay marriage. Society should be more worried about marriages without sex. No sex leads to more divorce and children suffering than same sex marriage."

Relief from their noisy quibbling arrived in the form of a fragrant risotto. We all sat down around the table, and the arguments were put aside. Quietly, everyone savored the long-awaited entrée. Afterwards, I cleared the table and Karen brought in dessert. "Ah, an old-fashioned hot fudge sundae," said Grant with an audible sigh. Karen smiled, confident of her ability to soothe and comfort her friends.

As I helped Karen load the dishwasher that night, I remember thinking about Roy and Grant, who were carrying their emotional baggage in completely different ways. Roy didn't live with his mentally ill mother, but still spent much of his life cleaning up the consequences of her illness.

She manifested full-blown psychotic episodes many times a year, usually claiming that she was pregnant by Immaculate Conception despite being 63 years-old. Sometimes she urinated on the floor, shouting that her water had broken, and demanding to go to the hospital to deliver. She frequently dialed 911 in the middle of the night for no logical reason.

Grant was also wrestling with skeletons in his closet. I was with

Grant when his best friend and cousin, Aaron, died a couple years ago. When Aaron, a vegetarian who jogged daily and who seemingly did everything right, developed a terminal illness, Grant was devastated by the capriciousness of it all. Most of the health problems doctors see in patients are the result of poor life-style choices: Lung disease from smoking, trauma from driving drunk, sexually transmitted disease, skin cancer from sun, and heart disease from poor diet all fall into this category. But, who knows why some people get an incurable form of lymphoma? Aaron was one of the unlucky ones, and a part of Grant had never forgiven the world for making that mistake.

For the first few hours after Aaron's death, I think Grant was actually relieved that his buddy no longer had to suffer. Death can be more painful for the loved ones left behind than for the person actually dying. Apparently, that wasn't the case for Aaron, who had fought hard through tremendous pain and torment. However, the reality of knowing he would never see Aaron again did sink in hard. The unearthly wailing that came out of Grant until sunrise sent shivers down my spine. Shortly afterwards, he started grinding his teeth in his sleep.

EIGHT

Notwithstanding that it was nearly midnight, fighting the intractable urge to call Klaus and find out anything new about the autopsy was agonizing. Karen and I tried to focus on anything other than Tarini. We tried reading in bed, knowing that sleep would probably be beyond our reach. We peeked at the hands of the bedside clock, which moved much too fast as we calculated the hours left to get some potential shuteye. I finally turned off my light and slid under the sheet; but the writhing sensations that started in my hips only aggravated the mental torture. I considered getting up for the third time to urinate, since it's always easier to sleep with an empty bladder, but then I worried that the increased physical demand of ambulating would only rev up my body more. Trying to displace my disturbed energy with thoughts about a recent vacation, the last movie watched – and of course, old Sesame Street episodes – didn't work. The insomnia made me feel homesick even though I was in my own bed. It was a feeling of displacement. Getting back into the warm dark silence of the womb seemed like the impossible cure.

Anyway, it appeared pointless to sleep since I'd just wake up with myself and all my problems in a few hours. My flannel pajamas felt too warm, and I envied the light-weight purple silk nightwear Karen had on. Her nightwear mirrored her smooth and thoughtful insights during tough situations. Karen is a very creative woman, but not an inventive woman. A creative person can take the facts and put them together in a sensible way. An interior designer puts together stuff like carpeting and furniture to cultivate an aesthetic appeal. An inventor actually makes a new piece of furniture or devises a new type of carpeting. Karen creates and leaves the inventing to others. After laying in bed in the dark another hour, I sensed she was still awake.

"Do you think she is in heaven, Karen?"

She flipped on the light, and then flipped out. "What? You're a Jew so you don't even believe in heaven and hell. I'm a recovering

Catholic. The one thing I believe is that those who claim that their way is the unrivalled truth, pollute the world."

"Really? You don't think about an afterlife at all?"

Two fluffy pillows rested between her head and our tufted-style headboard. I looked at her cute pug nose admiringly, but she didn't look at me. Instead, she continued to stare blankly at her hands.

"I do, but I don't let religious zealots define my beliefs. Just because some guy in a pointed hat says something is infallible, I'm not going to believe it. They are all hypocrites anyway. During my Catholic school graduation they wouldn't let a girl who was visibly pregnant march in the ceremony. They did let three girls whom everyone knew had had abortions partake in graduation. That's how their game works. It goes back to when the Pope wanted to kill Galileo for saying the Earth wasn't the center of the universe. It's all about scare tactics to force people to conform, and then eventually get their money. Heaven and hell are the same thing. It's a scare tactic to make people be the robots the church wants them to be, or else big daddy in the sky has a punishment waiting."

For a moment, I tried to imagine what form Tarini had taken. Maybe her molecules had a cosmic orgasm with the natural universe. Maybe she was in some other dimension we don't know about. Maybe there is a whole lot of nothing after death and she simply doesn't exist. I decided to stick with my vision of her in heaven.

"Yet, you still somehow believe in God?" I asked Karen.

"Yes I believe in God. I just don't believe one human is closer to God than another, or that we can only speak to God through an intermediary. Just because people consider themselves religious, it doesn't mean they get some special insight from the divinity about the afterlife."

It reminded me of something my father once said. I repeated it. "The ones who don't know, tell; the ones who know, can't tell."

"Not to mention the whole Messiah thing," she continued. "The universe is billions of years old. There are unlimited planets and stars. Despite infinite space and time, God decided two-thousand years ago to place his son in the image of a human being on our planet to save us? And we're still waiting for a second coming since he didn't fulfill the role of the Messiah the first time around? That isn't faith, Jerry. To me, that is delusional psychosis."

And with that she peered deep into my eyes. Life was progressing much faster since Karen moved out to Oregon. Time had proceeded with exaggerated slowness when I was alone. Not that being alone didn't have an upside, because it did. Goals, like medical school and residency, were easier to achieve since my energy was focused inward. Nevertheless, it was more fun to celebrate small successes with Karen than it was to celebrate big success alone.

"I'm going to marry you some day. Seriously, I am," I stated. That's the type of thing a guy will blurt out when the alien called love possesses the spirit. Anyway, I'd never find another woman like her who contained the entire full package. In the past I'd mistakenly felt similarly about other girlfriends. There were times I would have done anything to keep Tonya or Betsy from leaving me, but thank the Lord for unanswered prayers. The past was embarrassing to think about. Like a salmon returning to its river, I'd keep returning to those witches despite the harshness of the environment they created. Those girls were so cold at times, my tears nearly formed icicles. Besides, unlike former girlfriends, Karen actually thinks I'm sexy. Then again, she also thinks Prince is sexy. Perhaps when men reach a certain stature, even the ugly guys win. Being a geek will never be an aphrodisiac. Money rectifies that. Plenty of nerdy doctors have hot girlfriends, and at this point in my life, I'm o.k. with it. When I'm seen in public with Karen, it gives confidence to the legions of lonely oddball men.

"Shut up Jerry," Karen said, laughing as she placed her book on the nightstand. She mounted me like a saddle and sat on my stomach. Her long brown hair dropped down into my face so I could barely see. Then she started tickling me and said, "Tomorrow night I'll share with you my thoughts on marriage. My opinions on that are much stronger than my opinions on religion."

"You mean you don't even believe in good old Judeo-Christian monogamy?"

I lifted off her nightgown. That never got old. Every time Karen was naked I felt like a kid on the first night of Hanukah.

"Sure I do. I just don't believe in good old Judeo-Christian monotony."

NINE

In my dream that night, my Subaru morphed into a rusted 1972 Ford Pinto. I was in a tuxedo, on my way to pick up Karen for an important event of some sort, and engine oil came spraying out of the dash, soaking my tux.. Downshifting out of 5th gear, the car got stuck in reverse gear. I drove down the streets and highways in reverse, while oil blurred my glasses. After catching a glimpse of the baby Panda seat-belted in the back, I pressed down hard on the accelerator. It stuck, and the car continued to accelerate to twice the speed limit. I managed to wake up just before crashing into a woman who looked like a cross between Karen and Tarini.

Leaving for work, still agitated by the dream, I was soothed to find my Subaru properly functioning. As I drove towards the hospital, I analyzed the disturbing images of my dream. The oil maybe meant that I would strike it rich, perhaps in terms of an answer about Tarini. Or, maybe it cautioned me that the slightest spark would result in my combustion. Hard to say it symbolized anything, but soon enough time would reveal its plans. One thing was clear, my subconscious had sent out a warning to be careful.

I walked into Dr. Klaus Vanwaggen's office just after sunrise, but he wasn't there. Although I had told him to expect me at 8 a.m., I knew that pathologists usually start their days much earlier. That's because surgeons prefer to schedule cases early in the morning while they are fresh-thinking and awake. They need the pathologists to interpret the surgical slides on their microscopes while the operation is in process. That way they can let the surgeon know whether or not the diseased area was entirely removed.

Pathology has always seemed ghoulish to me. Very few things in medicine gross me out. Autopsies are essential for solving medical mysteries, but inopportunely I learned how they could undo me.

Every second-year medical student must participate in an autopsy as a graduation requirement. The pathology department supplied medical students throughout the year with autopsy pagers. You wear the pager a few days, and when it goes off you must come in to help perform the autopsy.

Starting in mid-December in my second year, I wore the pager for sixteen days straight, and it never rang. When it finally did, the timing was disastrous. I had been out celebrating New Year's Eve until 3 a.m. At 5:18 a.m. the damn thing rang louder than a Chinese gong next to my ear. If I ignored the pager or made an excuse that I hadn't heard it, I would have failed the class. Medical students are obsessive-compulsive when it comes to grades. Failure was never an option.

Walking the six blocks to the hospital on that dark and icy morning was difficult enough, but after slipping on the ice, half-drunk and half-hung-over, my horrendous migraine intensified. In the autopsy room, jarring bright lights shined over the draped body. Too bad sunglasses weren't allowed. I checked out the tag attached to the sheet covering the body. Someone had scrawled in sloppy ballpoint penmanship 'Case # 1984-00001'.

The pathology intern finally arrived at 7 a.m. I had been sitting on a cold, rusted stool for an hour waiting for her. That entire hour I spent staring at the sheet-covered corpse, and the gleaming knives and carving tools on a near-by table. I was praying I wouldn't have to get too involved in the whole thing. Perhaps I would be allowed just to observe the horror. No such luck. The perky intern turned to me and said, "Obviously the attending doc won't be coming in on New Year's Day. It's just the two of us."

She lifted the sheet off the body. It was a woman in her fifties, and by our measurements, five-feet tall and weighing 312 lbs. The intern took the large scalpel and made a swift incision from the bottom of the breastplate, through the abdomen, to the pubic bone just above the vagina. The yellow fat glistened like a golden chandelier under those bright lights. She made me spread and hold open the fresh wound. Thank God for latex gloves. She proceeded to cut deeper and deeper through the layers of fat until she got to the abdominal cavity housing the organs. Her arms were buried up past her elbows inside the obese abdomen. Nothing in my life could have prepared me for the odor when the bowels were cut. Dead bowel is the single worst smell that exists. Trust me.

The autopsy lasted about three hours. Surprisingly, and in spite of cold sweats and a woozy head, I didn't puke. My feet nearly gave out from under me on a few occasions. When I finally got home, I found bologna I'd left out on the counter from the night before. The thought of the grinding and mixing of muscle and fat to process and make the bologna was the last straw. I hurled sour beer vomit into the kitchen sink and spent the next hour with dry heaves. For a year I stayed completely sober, and I've permanently banned bologna from my diet. Like a wedding or high school graduation, that was a defining day in my life.

Although Klaus wasn't in his office, I knew he was somewhere in the building. I had parked right next to his old weather beaten Volkswagen. Until recently, the car backfired every few minutes with an incredibly loud explosion. Car alarms were constantly being triggered by that sorry excuse for an automobile. When the hospital administration gave him an ultimatum, after the Chief of Cardiology complained that two of his patients were so startled in the parking lot that they suffered heart attacks, he finally fixed it. Nobody looking at that car would have guessed the owner earned a six-digit salary.

I left an authentic German pewter beer stein engraved with scenes of Bavarian dancers on his desk. The stein had been sitting in my curio cabinet for years and was a gift from a German medical exchange student who had spent a month under my tutelage. Klaus was sure to love it. I was retreating from his office when I heard a toilet flush behind a door that I had always presumed was a closet. Dr. Vanwaggen walked out without washing his hands. Hospitals and restaurants are the place where hand washing is essential. Hospitals are filled with so much bacteria, I also wash my hands *before* I go the bathroom. Klaus didn't close the bathroom door behind him. The room quickly took on an odor of feces mixed with formaldehyde. He was not even slightly embarrassed, so I hypothesized he was hoping to be offensive enough to keep me from visiting in the future.

"You are early, Dr. Vize-man." He eyed the pewter stein without emotion.

"I want you to know I appreciate your help. This is a gift."

"In German, *gift* means poizon."

"Klaus, your tie is still draped over your right shoulder. You've got to remember that stuff after going to the bathroom."

He grunted and pulled the tie down.

"Pleaze, come back later. Zee autopzy iss not complete."

"What have you found so far, anything?"

"Ze only abnormality iss zome free fluid in ze abdominal cavity."

Klaus was not going to elaborate on that point without me pushing him. He sat down at his microscope and began adjusting the focus. I assumed he had looked at me for the last time that morning. One of the unpredictable things about Portland is the people. My ardent love for the city withstood my dislike of many of its citizens. There are very few native Portlanders, and I was accustomed to a diversity of mannerisms, but his personality drove me nuts.

"I thought free fluid in the abdominal cavity would be normal for a menstruating woman."

Whenever we get abdominal ultrasounds or CAT scans, the report for young women will often note incidental free abdominal fluid. When the ovary releases an egg each month, the ovary also releases free fluid.

"Ahh, zo zmart. I can't get anyting pazt you, Dr. Vize-man."

Klaus was being condescending. He knew these were facts every medical student would know.

"So you're not too worried about the fluid either?"

"I mozt zertainly am!" he hollered.

"Why? Was it not clear like ovarian fluid? Was it bloody? Was there a lot of fluid?" I was thinking of other possibilities that could have suddenly killed Tarini. Maybe she suddenly ruptured an appendix or burst her aorta.

"It vaz clear!" Klaus snapped, as he brandished one of his sporadic snarls that partially unmasked his crooked yellowing teeth.

"Oh for fucks sake!! Just tell me what is unusual about the fluid!"

"I do not appreciate your curzing. Your mutter should have taught you better. I demand you zpeak in a kinder and more professional fashion ven you addrezz me."

"Klaus, let's remember we are talking about a very good friend of mine. Now, please tell me what's abnormal about her abdominal fluid."

He sat staring into his microscope for a few more seconds, and loved every second of the annoying delay.

"She doezn't have any ovariez, Dr. Vize-man."

Now that was unusual. Free abdominal fluid is an abnormality unless it is from the ovaries. Obviously, Tarini had some serious illness. I was partially relieved that some sort of disease must have been the cause of her death. Anything was better than finding out she had been murdered.

"Were there inflammatory cells or blood in the fluid?"

"No."

"Was the cytology or cell line positive for cancer in the fluid?"

"No."

"Klaus, do you ever get tired of the twenty questions game? Just tell me what the fluid contained."

"I cannot."

He was really starting to piss me off. I knew I had to keep my cool or else he would get too much pleasure from dragging it on even longer. Of course he knew. He was a good pathologist. Even a bad pathologist can accurately identify the origin of body fluids. Instead of asking another question, I decided I would just stand there silently until he was ready to tell me the whole story. I stood there for about fifty seconds. Then the unthinkable happened. He leaned back from the microscope and made direct eye contact with me.

"Ze fluid did not originate from ze body. Zis vaz not human fluid."

"Fucking impossible, Klaus; you know it." He didn't show any sign of disagreeing. He looked as perplexed as me. There was no explanation. If you perforated your stomach from an ulcer and drank something, then there would be a foreign fluid in the abdomen. But stomach acid and blood would be present as well. Also, Dr, Vanwaggen did the autopsy himself. It would be hard to miss a perforated organ like the stomach or intestines. No doubt he also went back many times looking for that kind of possibility.

"You obviously checked the skin of her abdomen and back to rule out any injections or needle marks?"

"Of courze. Many timez."

"We have to get that fluid to a nuclear magnetic resonance machine to find out what it is."

He looked at me with pity, as if I was totally stupid. It was clear he already had pursued that avenue. Usually it takes a minimum of a day for that type of analysis to be completed. Klaus Vanwaggen shrugged his shoulders. The diagnostic challenge had captivated his attention.

TEN

While driving to Grant's house, I reflected on Mother and my career. After all, they are the two endeavors that occupy the majority of my time. The preliminary autopsy results meant I wasn't paranoid. That was a relief, because the one thing I tried to avoid all my life was behaving like my mother.

My mother always finds blame in every health tragedy. She frequently recounted stories about friends who were admitted into the hospital, and how doctors subsequently ended up killing them. The lethal nature of the disease would be inconsequential.

Last week Mother called to tell me about her friend, Jane. "They found Jane had breast cancer that spread to the brain. She was in the hospital only four days, had a biopsy and died. They killed her! It would be better she never went to the hospital."

"But Mom, breast cancer with metastasis to the brain can cause death very quickly. Sometimes only days."

"Nonsense. Besides, they should stop the spread before it gets to that point."

"Mom, nobody would ever die of cancer if we could always pick it up at the earliest stage. Many people are in the late stages when they present with symptoms."

"Jerry, you should tell your patients to prevent the cancer in the first place with vitamins. And I don't think you are getting enough vitamins. Your immune system needs vitamins, or you too will get cancer."

"Ma, there is evidence out there showing the opposite in megavitamin users. Tumors can grow faster because the cancer cells are fed by abundant nutrition. The cells then have an easier time dividing faster. The tumor grows faster."

"I'm not only talking about vitamins, Jerry. Don't try and give me a conniption. I'm only telling you good nutrition in general will prevent cancer."

You simply don't try to teach a Jewish mother about food and vitamins. At some point in the conversation you must give her the victory. At least by that time, the blame had shifted from the hospital to the doctors to the vitamins.

For a physician to be blamed for life's miseries when you were doing your best to help is demoralizing. I have yet to meet a doctor who intentionally hurt a patient. Sometimes it can be easy to exhibit bitterness about everything. It just felt like the whole world was against me that year. My mother, higher malpractice rates, increased paperwork, claims rejections, aggressive pharmaceutical reps, prior authorizations, the uninsured, the possibility that Tarini was killed by one of my friends in my house... All this was making me frantic.

I sat in the car for ten minutes trying to get up my courage to ring Grant's doorbell, and weighed the different remarks I might use to start our conversation. Something. Anything that would be meaningful and compassionate. He had really loved Tarini.

Getting out of my car, I decided that if I continued to live in Portland, I'd get that laser eye surgery. The light drizzle, as usual, blurred my glasses. Wiping rain from my glasses thirty times a day was so irritating.

It was a slow saunter from the car to the door. Grant's car blocked the driveway, so I made my way across his front yard. The ground was squishy, but my shoes did not get any mud on them. The fecund soil combined with Oregon's crying clouds keeps the vegetation lush year-round resulting in the grass forming an impenetrable barrier between the dirt and my shoes.

Grant didn't answer the bell, so I knocked and let myself in. He sat on his brown, fine-grained Italian leather couch with his back to me. He turned, and with a hand signal, motioned for me to sit down next to him. As I sat down I could hear that abrasive sound of him grinding his teeth. All the window curtains were shut to prevent anyone from observing his misery, but brilliantly colored Peruvian paintings covered his walls. I wondered if they provided unwelcome cheer for someone in mourning. The oil paintings were more than just art. The Inca-inspired canvases were also memories of an adventurous vacation Tarini and Grant took to Machu Picchu last summer.

"I don't know what to say, Grant."

We both kept quiet for a while and stared at the beige carpet.

It was not an uncomfortable silence, but I felt a deep-seated desire to know what he was thinking. "You once told me you would never get married. Did you ever consider proposing to Tarini?"

Softly he replied, "Naturally, I did consider that several times."

I knew Grant was scared to marry again. One divorce was more than he ever wanted. Also, his father had instilled in him skepticism towards that institution. The old man had struck it rich in real estate, was thrice divorced, and pursued the life of a playboy. His father also had a pilot's license and was a competent yachtsman. His patriarchal advice to Grant had always been, *if it flies, floats, or fucks – rent it.*

"Grant. Did you and Tarini ever talk about having kids?"

Grant hunched forward a bit in the couch to get more comfortable.

He gave me a Dirty Harry type glance and said, "Tarini would not have been able to have children so it was not a topic we addressed. Anyway, we weren't even married."

"She couldn't have children?" I pretended to be surprised.

"She had a bilateral oopherectomy for dysplastic ovarian cysts. Her mother and grandmother died of ovarian cancer. She figured her pre-malignant condition would turn malignant, and she didn't want to take that chance. Tarini never wanted another child anyway." He started tapping his fingers rhythmically on the armrest of the couch.

"What? I'm sorry. I thought you just said *another child*. Tarini doesn't have a child. Right?"

Having gotten to know Tarini quite well in the past year, I felt certain there was no child in her life.

"That's correct. She doesn't have a child. But, she *did* have a child."

Bombshell!! Absorb the shock. Keep composure. It felt like the Earth rocked so hard the ground became wobbly. None of my good friends had kids, although Earl came close to having one. Once, on a steamy evening when he and his college girlfriend found themselves without a condom, Earl tried using a potato chip bag instead. It didn't do the job, but his girlfriend miscarried a month later.

"If, um – did. Can – can you explain that to me a little better?"

"It's not something she would have talked with anybody about on a casual basis, Jerry."

"Yeah, O.K. It's just she never even slightly dropped a hint.

Young women in their thirties who have had a child usually say something. From what I'm gathering, it sounds like the child died?"

He gazed at me and nodded his head. "Yes. Tarini had a baby in college. The typical young girl who made a mistake story. The father abandoned ship halfway into the second trimester. She worked hard, getting through college as a single mom. Never could afford a babysitter. The college had a daycare she could use during class hours, but otherwise she had little support. Friends were not plentiful since she was a dedicated premed student and had a baby. Hard to have an active social life with those obligations.

"One night she was studying late for a test. After missing both lunch and dinner that day, she decided to get a sandwich at the deli half a block away. The baby was sleeping. It was only four months old. She was gone less than ten minutes. She left the baby sleeping on its back, the position recommended by pediatricians in order to prevent SIDS. When she came back to her apartment, the baby was blue."

"Oh my God! That is one of the most tragic stories I've ever heard." It also proved my privately held theory that Tarini was one of those natural beauties who could maintain a sexy figure even after childbirth.

"Needless to say, children were not something we discussed often. Most likely she would not have been interested in having another child even if she still had her ovaries." Grant's eyes glistened. He was on the verge of tears. Something inside of me wished that the baby had survived. Tarini's legacy to all of us would have been more than a well-carved headstone.

She always seemed so content with life. As if her dreams were realized every day because she kept her dreams small and attainable. Maybe Tarini was purposefully hiding her sadness like a sorrowful clown that paints on a happy face. Alternatively, she may have been genuinely happy and perchance had overcome the trials life dispensed. I'll never know for sure.

The conversation with Grant had numbed me. It's a cliché, but you never know people as well as you think you do. Who else was hiding behind a mask? Did I really know Grant and Earl? Was the hippy Roy capable of homicide? Was Karen deceiving me? Did I know myself?

I was sober, but left Grant's house in no emotional condition to drive. The speedometer read 60 mph. The speed limit was 45. Driving above the speed limit was my norm, and only on rare occasions did I follow the posted limits. Those were the times when I've slowed down enough to smell the roses and lived life as it should be lived - without urgency - not feeling that something is being missed. Those are the sporadic moments when you notice the frantic driver tailing the slow elderly driver. You notice your surroundings and feelings. Like a Buddhist, the journey, not the destination, assumes value.

The realization I had been driving at 60 mph was my first indication that no major new insights regarding Tarini would materialize. If it had been a time when introspection and reflection were about to transpire, I would have been below the speed limit. Forcing myself to slow down would not have helped matters. Either things would come to me naturally, or I was going to have to set time aside to work at solving the tasks ahead of me. Ben Franklin said that genius is 99% perspiration and 1% inspiration. Solving the death of Tarini would be all perspiration. Nothing was meant to just fall in my lap. As my father often told me, *it's O.K. to hope for miracles, but not to rely on them.*

At that moment my only major insight was that I had gotten lost. Where the hell had I been driving for the last twenty minutes? I had no direction. No plan. I worried that my mind was a temple of chaos slipping into the vacant chasm of senselessness. A strategy was crucial.

Flashbacks of classic films like *The Thin Man* and old Charlie Chan movies raced through my head. A part of me wanted to act like an amateur sleuth and get everyone who was present at the dinner party back together again in one room to try to hash out the mystery. Fortunately, I realized how ludicrous it would be to pretend my title was *Dr. Jerry Weissman – Ace Detective*. Interrogating my friends was not an option. I've always loathed false accusers like Joseph McCarthy, and had little interest in taking part in anything along those lines with my posse. To interrogate the innocent is nearly the same as falsely accusing.

I was lost, but was that all bad? Moses and the Israelites were lost in the desert for forty years. Eventually, they found their Jerusalem. Serendipity baby! Or was it?

A few years ago, my fair skinned, redheaded Israeli cousin, a Special Forces sergeant who had spent years training and fighting in that same desert, took me hiking in the Golan Heights on a 114 degree Fahrenheit day. As the sweat dripped down his face, he laughed. "Damn Moses! If he would just have kept walking another forty years we would be in Switzerland skiing right now."

Whatever one's take was on Moses, one thing was clear. I needed to solve Tarini's death in much less than forty years, and I couldn't rely on serendipity.

ELEVEN

The next morning Klaus was not in his office when I arrived at 5 o'clock. I even opened the bathroom door to be sure.

I went up to the ICU to check on my patient with terminal heart disease. During the night, the cardiothoracic surgeon had placed her on an aortic balloon pump. Basically, it's a long sausage shaped tube that is inserted into a person's biggest artery, the aorta. As it inflates and deflates many times a minute, it pushes blood around the body, but it's never as effective as nature's greatest pump – the heart.

The patient's daughter was in her mother's room, sleeping on a cot the nurses had provided. I woke her up.

"It looks like your mom was placed on a balloon pump last night."

"I think it gonna help her heart," she replied.

"Well it's not actually going to help her heart. It actually acts as her heart when her heart is too weak to pump blood around the body itself."

"Uh-huh, as long as it gonna help her heart, don't matter to me what it does."

Some days provide few incentives to continue the frustrating practice of medicine. In college I started out as a music major. Kicking down the blues with your drinking buddies seemed much more appealing. The reason I didn't follow through in that direction was on my mother's advice. *"Jerry, be a musician if that's what you want. All I'm saying is be a doctor on the side,"* she would say at regular intervals. The guidance was ultimately very good. My musician friends from college have been struggling hard to make ends meet.

I turned to my patient's daughter, and tried again. "I must tell you that it really is not going to reverse her heart disease. The balloon does not make the heart stronger. Usually aortic balloon pumps are used as a bridge to more definitive therapy such as a heart transplant."

Why did I just refer to the device as an 'aortic balloon pump'? The term was sure to confuse this already confused woman. Keep it simple, I thought. 'Balloon' would have been a much better way to describe the equipment. Even those who've taken anatomy rarely remember where the aorta is located unless they are medical professionals. This woman definitely had not had anatomy. How would I have felt if someone were trying to explain aeronautics to me in terms I'd never heard? Well, I'd feel just like I do when car mechanics take me for what I'm worth at auto repair shops, using terms I never understand.

That was the problem. She regarded me as the equivalent of an auto mechanic.

Moreover, many African-Americans have never quite trusted the American medical system. There was good reasoning behind that. Most have heard of the obscene Tuskegee syphilis experiment conducted by white doctors who allowed African Americans to reach the end stages of syphilis. It took place at a time when there was an excellent and easy-to-use cure available (penicillin). In fact, the experiment that started in 1932 only ended when the *Washington Star* broke the story in July 1972. Those men died in unnecessary, unrelenting misery. Not to mention the wives that got infected, and then the children born with syphilis to those infected women. A class action suit awarded $10 million to the families that suffered from the atrocious event. It may sound like a lot of money, but considering that Dow Corning Corporation had to pay $3.2 billion in 1998 to women that electively received silicone breast implants, the Tuskegee reparations are shameful.

Studies in well-respected scientific publications such as the New England Journal of Medicine show that degrees of racism are still present in medicine. For instance, African Americans in severe pain are less likely to get morphine than white people with the same disease process. African Americans who have heart disease are less likely to get cardiac bypass surgery than white Americans with the same degree of disease.

The daughter of my patient didn't care where the aorta was, or what it does. She cared about mom. Telling her to accept her mother's death was like telling me to accept Tarini's death. Those things do not happen easily.

Nevertheless, this was a different situation. Tarini was already dead. Unfortunately, the sad reality was that my patient was not only going to die, she was also basically dead already. Miracles do happen in hospitals, but in this patient's case, it would have been nearly the same as raising Lazarus.

Just because technology exists does not mean it should always be used. The technology that kept her mom partly alive cost tens of thousands of dollars a day. Just as important, the strain of a prolonged, uncomfortable death was taking its toll on the visibly shaken daughter. The longer her mother's suffering went on, the longer it would upset her for years to come.

"I'll come by to check on your mother later."

"Thank you, Doctor."

TWELVE

Walking through the dark basement toward the pathology department, I felt like a spaceman buckled in for take-off. An astronaut is acutely aware he is not the most important part of the lift-off. The team that built the ship is more responsible for the outcome of the mission. If the engineers have a flawed design, the rocket is doomed, no matter how flawlessly the pilot performs.

Like it or not, Klaus was the key member of my team. Unless he found the exact cause of Tarini's death, the mission would not be a success. He was aggravating and vile, but I wasn't going to let him unhinge me. If a forensic criminal pathologist was not available for the case, then Klaus was the next best thing. Sometimes you've got to appreciate and trust in what you have. Besides, alone I was just a fragile snowflake, but snowflakes that stick together can construct mighty glaciers.

"What do you have for me, Klaus?"

Under my breath I recited a short prayer that he had unraveled the mystery.

"Not ready, Doctor Vize-man."

"What is the origin of the fluid?"

A frustrating feeling was rising inside me. It was like trying to run fast, but finding myself in the same spot.

"Not ready. Come back in four hourz," he replied, without looking at me. His hand waved me off, as if by old habit.

I headed to Medical Records to complete the required, but never ending, charting and signatures. As always, when I was done with charting I went to the 'Confidential Case Review' section of the records department. As vice-chairman of the Internal Medicine department, I was required to chart-review my colleagues for possible medical mistakes. Each department administration did its own reviews. Surgery reviewed the surgical deaths. Pharmacy and Therapeutics reviewed all medication errors. Such review procedures persist as a standard in nearly every hospital in the country, as a way to improve quality control. Peer review has to be completed in a highly confidential manner. If word got out that a case was being internally reviewed, it would be only minutes before some lawyer would call a family member to suggest there had been malpractice. The truth was that most chart reviews did not show malpractice. Bad outcomes do not signify poor care. Diseases progress and people die. Nothing can ultimately stop that.

From the hospital's well-organized shelf, I pulled out the Internal Medicine charts. Carrying them to the desk, I glanced over and noticed a chart further down the shelf with the name Phil Michaelson. It was in the Oncology section for chart review. Phil Michaelson was a local car dealer celebrity. You couldn't watch an hour of television without seeing his face or hearing one of his sales pitches. There was Phil Michaelson Chevrolet and Pontiac, Phil Michaelson Subaru, Phil Michaelson Used Trucks, Phil Michaelson whatever-the-hell car you desire.

I had read in the papers a few weeks earlier that he had died of lung cancer. He had been one of Earl's patients. Earl had mentioned that Phil Michaelson was actually a nice guy who was not nearly as annoying as the ads that promoted him on television.

Curiosity got the best of me. I pulled the chart to see what the case was about, undeterred by the fact that it was unethical to read private records of a case in a department I had no authority to review. I reasoned I'd only peek for a second. If someone caught me with the chart I'd say it was accidentally put in the Internal Medicine file, and then perhaps I'd scold the medical records worker for not properly putting it in the Oncology section to begin with.

To my surprise, the hospital's legal department had already reviewed the chart and prioritized the case as high risk. They had left a note explaining potential areas of liability for the hospital and doctors. It was an interesting situation. Phil Michaelson had paid out of pocket for one of those full body screening CAT scans, which are controversial for many reasons besides the fact they cost about a thousand dollars for each screen. Not only do they give the patient about fifty times the dose of radiation as an average chest x-ray, but to be effective they need to be repeated each year. Consequently, there is eventually a huge radiation build-up that in itself could cause cancer. Most important, abnormal findings are usually not of life-threatening significance. Just as our skin develops blemishes as it ages, so do our organs. Most of the bumps and rough spots on aging skin are not cancer. Similarly, in an otherwise asymptomatic individual, most blemishes and nodules in aging organs like the lungs are not malignant. However, the only way to tell for sure is to get a biopsy of any abnormality that shows up on the scan. That sometimes requires open chest surgery, which is dicey stuff that always carries a mortality risk.

The overwhelming majority of the time those biopsy results are found to be benign. Therefore, many patients undergo unnecessary and risky surgery. Phil Michaelson was a fifty-seven-year-old lifelong smoker whose scan had shown a tiny nodule on his right lung. Earl had advised him to wait on surgery, and to get another CAT scan in six months to see if the nodule was growing. Unfortunately for Phil and Earl, the nodule had grown. Not slowly like most lung cancer. There were tumors on both sides of the chest on the second CAT scan.

In modern medicine, a lung malignancy is only surgically curable if there is a single tumor nodule on one side of the chest. Once there is more than one nodule, the tumor has obviously undergone major spread. Chemotherapy with tumor toxic medications becomes the only option. It almost never cures advanced lung cancer.

Phil Michaelson underwent chemo for eight months with no improvement. A week prior to his death he went to see his primary care physician. That doctor mentioned to Phil and his wife that if the oncologist had pursued a biopsy of the lung after the first CAT scan, the cancer would have been detected earlier, and it might have been curable. Phil and his wife already knew that. The new implication by the primary care doctor was that the oncologist had exceedingly erred in his decision making.

The Michaelsons never went back to see Earl. After his death, the wife hired a lawyer.

Why hadn't Earl shared that with me? Lawsuits are incredibly worrisome for doctors. They can ruin you financially and emotionally even if you win the case. Often, physicians can't get malpractice insurance again even if they simply have been named in a lawsuit.

My heart sank in sympathy for Earl. All he had tried to do was help someone who developed a deadly disease caused by the patient's own risky smoking habit. In hindsight, an early biopsy would have been the right call. But Earl and I had seen plenty of cases where it was the wrong call. People can either get injured or die from doctors working up something that is not cancer. It was just bad luck that this was such a fast spreading tumor.

Who was the jackass primary care physician that implicated Earl? It didn't say on the hospital lawyer's note. Defense lawyers on a hospital legal team are smart enough never to mention the name of any physician that isn't already named in a suit.

I searched the chart for the primary doctor's name. I wanted to avoid sharing cases with that doctor in the future. Finally, I found the original referral letter from the primary care doctor to Earl. The note was signed by Dr. Tarini Parvan.

THIRTEEN

A few anxious hours passed.

"What do you have for me, Klaus?"

He looked concerned. Klaus never, ever, looks concerned.

I felt a deep-pitted sinking sensation in my stomach, my body's involuntary response to the bad news Klaus was about to reveal -- a physical sensibility most commonly associated with roller-coaster rides or falling backwards after leaning too hard on a chair. It was the same apprehensive feeling I got the day I was stuck on a broken hospital elevator for three hours with a patient suffering from diarrhea-predominant irritable bowel syndrome.

"It iss vec," Klaus uttered. He disclosed the information in the quietest voice I'd ever heard him use.

I slumped into his black leather desk chair, glad it was conveniently behind me.

"Of course… vec," I mumbled.

"I shall call ze polize," said Klaus.

It's not that a similar thought hadn't crossed my mind. Right after we found Tarini dead, I had considered calling a new acquaintance, retired Detective Frankie Russo. I remembered him feeling indebted to me for saving his drug damaged brother a few weeks earlier, and how he had offered to do me a favor anytime I needed it. But I wasn't sure he could be trusted. The last thing I wanted was an unnecessary public commotion that could affect all our careers.

In an odd, roundabout way, I also happened to be thinking about Russo in the hours preceding Tarini's death. The olfactory system is one of the most ancient parts of the brain. Smell helps us detect essentials for survival, facilitating the search for food or avoidance of poisons. That is why odor has such an important role in triggering memory recall. On Tarini's last night of life, at my house, a lingering odor of skunk had triggered my memory.

While Karen and Tarini took turns stirring the risotto, Iko had ambled over to me, asking to be petted. Smelling the faint remnants of the skunk that had sprayed her a few weeks earlier had kindled my recollection of the night I met Russo. I had let Iko out into the backyard just before bedtime, and promptly learned that skunks are nocturnal creatures that enjoy living under my house deck. Hours were spent showering and scrubbing Iko, trying to get the skunk oil out of her fur. While it may not have been as bad as performing a fresh autopsy of dead bowel, it was a disgusting task. Scrubbing a dog freshly sprayed with fetid skunk musk is extremely irritating to the mucous membranes, and my throat became red and irritated. By the time the job was finished, or at least eighty percent finished, I was able to squeeze in just a couple hours of sleep before it was time to wake up for work. The thought of facing twenty-four hours straight of on-call hospital duty was daunting.

There is a hospital rule of thumb that when you are well rested and energetic, the wards will be quiet, even boring. When you're fatigued, sick people will stream through the doors like an assembly line. Sure enough, it was during my long, sleep-deprived shift after de-skunking Iko, that one of my most unusual cases arrived in the ER.

Dr. Stover had refused to give me a good reason over the phone why a certain elderly man needed admission to the hospital, but urged me to come down to the ER and hear the story myself. Stepping into the examining area, I saw a man who was clearly haggard and emaciated. He seemed agitated and was shivering despite being swathed in blankets. Standing next to his bed was another senior citizen, with peppered grey hair and bearing a resemblance to the patient, but who, in contrast, was well groomed and marginally overweight.

I introduced myself to the patient and began my usual line of questioning.

"Sir, what made you come to the hospital tonight?"

"My foolish asshole brother!"

"How are you feeling?"

"Most splendid."

A pattern I've noticed since my first day in practice was being adhered to. The sick think they are healthy, and the truly healthy are convinced they are sick.

"Is there anything I can do for you?"

"In point of fact, there is, young man. Leave me alone!"

In between my questions, he would fall asleep. He seemed disoriented. I was forced to get the patient's medical history from the brother, who introduced himself as Frankie Russo.

Russo described his brother as a former English literature professor at a major university. Well-published, he had lectured throughout the country, then retired five years ago and moved to Mexico with his male lover. He planned to enjoy his remaining years with cheap drinks and drugs that can only be found south of the border. Soon after arriving in Mexico, he developed a cocaine habit. He was smart enough never to inject the cocaine. His method of choice was to dissolve the cocaine in water and give himself cocaine enemas. The rapid absorption through the colon provided a rush almost as fast as the intravenous route.

As Frankie recounted his brother's story to me, the patient periodically opened his eyes and cursed his brother. Frankie returned the honor by screaming back, "Shut the fuck up, you stupid buffoon! I'm talking with the doctor. Capeesh?"

Like all cocaine addicts, my patient had become paranoid. From Mexico, he had repeatedly telephoned his brother to describe how a special branch of the CIA was hunting him. Frankie had pleaded with him during every phone call to come back to the States.

The patient interrupted his brother's recounting of the story. "Why would I want to come back to this elitist pig country where there are no human freedoms?"

"What, like Mexico is a place of freedom?" Frankie yelled back. "Just shut your goddamn mouth while I tell the doctor what he needs to know. Sorry, Doctor, my brother used to be an upstanding citizen, but he's lost all sense of respect. I'm just thankful my parents, God bless their souls, are not here to witness this travesty."

Frankie explained that his brother had an accountant in Tennessee who managed his retirement funds. Each week he'd have money wired from Tennessee to Mexico. The accountant called Frankie several weeks earlier to warn him that the wire transfers had been rapidly escalating in amount. The funds would run out in three months at the current pace of things.

Frankie went down to Mexico to rescue his almost destitute, delusional, addicted baby brother, who had, fatefully, become my patient. When he got to Mexico, Frankie noticed holes every few feet in all the walls of his brother's new house. Using a chisel and hammer, his brother had attempted to find "the bugs" he was certain the CIA had planted as listening devices in his hacienda. His brother was convinced that the CIA was running a five-hundred-man sting operation to frame his lover, who had recently been arrested for prostitution and was serving time in a Mexican jail.

There was nothing Frankie Russo had been able to say to convince him to return to the U.S. The guy was not stupid enough to willingly leave a location with a constant and relatively cheap cocaine supply.

Frankie decided to kidnap his brother. In Mexico, you do not need a doctor's prescription to obtain medicines. Frankie went to the town pharmacy and obtained a bottle of Zyprexa, a sedating psychiatric medicine. He mixed twenty times the usual dose into a frozen margarita, and gave it to his unsuspecting brother, who quickly became oblivious to his surroundings.

Frankie then drove my patient to the airport and purchased two airplane tickets for the first flight to the U.S., which just happened to be going to Portland International Airport. A nice bit of luck for Frankie, who had been a cop in Portland before retirement. Frankie convinced the airline that his extremely lethargic brother had suffered a major stroke and was expected in Portland for medical care. When they arrived, the U.S. customs agent appropriately called an ambulance, which brought them directly to my hospital's emergency room.

Legally and ethically I had no training on how to proceed. Frankie assured me the cops were on his side. He handed me his card and told me, "If I can help you out in any way, Doc, no matter what the trouble, give me a call." It amazes me how many people hand out business cards to doctors taking care of their family members. Usually they are investment advisors, or house painters, and desire your business. Frankie Russo's card is the only one I ever kept, thank God.

I paged the on-call psychiatrist who had admitted Frankie's delusional brother to the psychiatric ward. A few days later the psychiatrist paged me to say I would need to come and transfer the patient to the intensive care unit. Frankie's brother had become short of breath and developed fevers. He had most likely aspirated saliva into his lungs during his many hours of being unconscious without a gag reflex to cough and clear the throat. He had a serious pneumonia. The results of the HIV testing I ordered in the ER had also come back positive for AIDS. He did recover from pneumonia, and by the time he left the hospital he was less delusional, and scared enough to embrace the concept of sobriety. Frankie was grateful, and reaffirmed his appreciation to me numerous times.

Seeing the problems others face can make my own problems seem petty and irrelevant. Things such as my dog getting skunked become trivial. I have one of the few jobs where dealing with all of the world's insanity actually makes me more balanced.

"Don't call the police, Klaus. Don't even think about it!" I exclaimed, half-warning and half-begging.

Someone in my house had committed murder, and surely we would all be suspects. I could picture the headlines:

PROMINENT PORTLAND DOCTORS QUESTIONED IN MURDER

Our lives and careers would be ruined. The case would take the police years to solve, if ever. They wouldn't get even as far as we had already gotten. There is a Yiddish saying - *der oilem iz a goilem - the masses are asses*. The murderer in this case had, and would continue to outsmart the masses, I believed.

"I need forty-eight hours, Klaus. That's it. I'll have it solved. If I don't, you can call the police at that time. You know I'm more likely than the police to solve this."

"There are rulez, Dr. Vize-man."

"Forty-eight hours, Klaus! The police won't get anything done in that amount of time other than arrest some of us. Just tell the police two days from now that you just got the results. You have nothing to lose. You'll never be a suspect in this case. Please."

"It iz nine in ze morning. At nine in ze morning on Turzday I vill call ze polize."

"Thanks, Klaus. I owe you big time. I really do."

I had one last question.

"How did the vec get inside Tarini?"

"It vaz juzt above ze dentate line."

FOURTEEN

Envisioning the nightmarish way Tarini had died horrified me. Vecuronium was genius. Going above the dentate line showed a particular cunning and lack of feeling on the killer's behalf. Lack of feeling, because we cannot feel anything above the dentate line.

The dentate line is an anatomical location all humans possess. The last 12 centimeters of the large intestine is called the rectum. If you stick your finger in your rectum, after about one centimeter you would be above the dentate line. There are zero pain nerves above the dentate line. There are pressure nerves, which are different from pain nerves. A person can feel miserable 'pressure' and fullness when the rectum is full of feces, but won't feel 'sharp' pain. If you've ever felt sharp pain while passing a large bowel movement, it was sharp pain that occurred as the feces traveled below the dentate line. That is why doctors classify hemorrhoids as either *internal* hemorrhoids or *external* hemorrhoids. The classification is dependent on the point of origin of the problem. If the hemorrhoidal tissue originates above the dentate line, it is classified as an internal hemorrhoid, and they never cause pain. External hemorrhoids originate below the dentate line, and can really hurt a lot. The killer could have injected Tarini with a needle above the dentate line and she would not have felt sharp pain.

In the last decade hospitals began using protective syringes to safeguard doctors and nurses from needle sticks. With a slight twist of the syringe they can expose the needle for injection. Another twist retracts the needle into the syringe so workers aren't exposed to dirty needles.

Whoever killed Tarini must have stuck a protective syringe into her rectum and then exposed the needle to inject her with vec. There would be no other way to easily get a needle in there without a major yelp. A small plastic syringe would feel similar to a small finger. If she didn't mind that sort of thing during sex, she would probably have figured it was her partner being kinky. Klaus had found only one tiny needle puncture above the dentate line internally.

The Other Face Of Murder

Vecuronium is a paralytic agent used every day in every hospital. Vecuronium is based on a poison called *curare* which is found in tropical South America. The native Indians, who make curare by boiling bark scrapings of the *Strychnos toxifera* plant with a native species of venomous ants, dip the tips of their blowgun darts into the curare. It completely paralyzes the muscles so animals cannot move. This includes the respiratory muscles. Heart muscle is the only muscle not paralyzed by curare and pharmaceutically manufactured Vecuronium. The medication is used in surgery to keep the body totally still, except for the movement of breathing created by the ventilator.

Vecuronium does not inhibit pain. It only paralyzes. Once in a while you'll read in the press about someone claiming they were awake during surgery and felt excruciating pain. Those very rare cases occur when the anesthesiologist paralyzes the patient with Vecuronium, but forgets to sedate the patient with other drugs. The patient would not be able to move or protest. Vecuronium does not alter awareness. In those terrible cases, the patient would be awake and feeling every slice of the surgery.

Tarini must have been awake and alert during her ordeal, I reasoned. She must have heard the conversation going on outside the pantry door. She was paralyzed and had to be suffocating. If we had been brave enough to open the door, we could have breathed for her with mouth-to-mouth resuscitation. The Vecuronium would have worn off in about fifteen minutes, and she would have been able to tell us who had tried to kill her. It's hard to say how long she was alert before the lack of oxygen induced a black out. Tarini probably heard the dog barking, and hoped she would be saved at any moment by one of us.

FIFTEEN

In a single morning Klaus had cracked open the case. It was murder, and the method of murder had been established. I believed Earl, that slug, had left a trail of slime and motives, but I needed to hear it from his mouth. The entire scheme wouldn't be fully believable unless he admitted it to me.

Having just forty-eight hours before Klaus would notify law enforcement added an element of pressure to the scenario.

I wasn't too afraid of Earl. It seemed unlikely my friend would be violent towards me. On the other hand, he had already been capable of murder once. Being much bigger and tougher than me did make him endowed to beat me in a fight. If he had been motivated to bump off Tarini over a lawsuit, avoiding jail or the electric chair would be an even stronger incentive to kill me. I hoped violence could be avoided, but just in case I had to be prepared to take matters into my own hands: I needed a gun. Obtaining the extra protection appeared justifiable. Unsure of the nature of the job I was about to undertake, it made perfect sense to have a variety of options at my disposal.

Besides, I knew Earl owned guns. His grandmother had bequeathed to him a collection of antique guns along with a Confederate uniform, all in excellent condition. She had hoped he'd make good use of his inheritance when, someday, the South would rise again. Confronting him without self–protection would be illogical, on my part.

Where do you get a gun?

Wal-Mart sounded like a reasonable option, but after I picked out my weapon, the salesman informed me about the five-day waiting period before I could take it home. He referred to it as the 'Brady Law,' named after the White House Press Secretary who took a bullet in the head during the President Reagan assassination attempt. I remembered hearing about it, but hadn't cared much one way or another in the past. You don't need a permit to buy a gun in Oregon, but you do have to wait. Two days was all I had. Klaus would not hold out for the Brady Law.

Every city has its seedy areas. In Portland, when you needed to get things done under the table, you headed for the Beaverton-Hillsdale highway. Just outside the southwest city limits, the highway runs through a place called Beaverton, which is basically, a strip mall for every taste and distaste. K-Mart next to a strip club; Sushi restaurants and record stores facing porno shops, etc. Just like Scottsdale has become part of Phoenix, and Berkeley has fused with Oakland, Beaverton was becoming lumped together with Portland.

Just a week prior to searching for a gun, I had been cruising that exact section of asphalt. I was driving up and down the roadway trying to make a decision between burgers and tacos. When that is your biggest dilemma, be thankful. Now, it was maddening to feel that every neuronal tract in my head was preoccupied with life and death issues.

After a stop at the Wells Fargo ATM to get more cash, I located a shabby looking pawnshop, which looked perfect for my needs. It was next door to Cheap Rides Bike Shop, which triggered the memory of our last conversation with Tarini at the dinner party before we went to bed.

Our party had been an anniversary celebration commemorating my third year in Portland. I had traveled from the American heartland and discovered a city full of surprises. I had assumed that Portland was named for its waterfront port, which allows easy access to the Pacific Ocean, but the reality was different. When the two men who settled that piece of northwest America, Francis Pettygrove and A.J. Lovejoy, could not agree on a name they flipped a coin. Pettygrove won, and named the infant city after his hometown of Portland, Maine, which actually had been named for its commercial port. Had Lovejoy won, he would have named it after his hometown, Boston. I've sometimes wondered what the original Indian name was for my newly adopted city.

Karen subsequently joined me in Oregon. We did the long distance relationship commute for a year so that she could complete a fellowship she had back in Ohio. Karen's broad, warm smile, lights up her attractive face and my spirit. Like most guys, looks are important to me, but combined with her perfect balance of humor and self-confidence, I found Karen irresistible. Besides, it helped having a tall, physically strong woman around in case a piece of furniture needed to be moved or a fallen tree needed to be cleared from the lawn. Although laid back, Karen could be a bit saucy, often going out on an edge to make her point understood. I was glad I got to Portland ahead of her so that I could establish some friends. Just about all my friends eventually end up liking her better than me. That has never made me overly jealous, but puts me in awe.

Grant, Tarini, Karen and I had made a frequent foursome exploring the restaurants and clubs in town. Just before bed and the subsequent crash that changed our lives, Karen and Tarini were in the kitchen planning a bike ride for later in the week. Plans and intentions that never transpired.

Big Bob's Pawnshop and Jewelry Store conveyed the right ambience. The interior had laminated fake wood walls and scuffed linoleum floors. A layer of sawdust covered the tools that were on sale. Neither the person that pawned them nor the pawnshop owner cared enough to clean them. Big Bob's store had the aura of being a front for a seedier establishment. Even the average thrift-store customer would snub the lack of dignity of the merchandise there.

"I need a gun," I explained to the huge, balding pawn broker whose Harley T-shirt barely covered his belly.

"What for?" he asked. He stood behind a Plexiglas counter about twenty feet from me. I couldn't see his hands. A collection of rifles were mounted on the wall behind him. He was chewing tobacco, and brown spit clung to areas of his graying ragged beard.

"My own business."

"There's a five-day mandatory wait, my friend," he said.

"I need one right now." That 'Brady Law' was really pissing me off. Ironically, it was meant exactly for people like me. A 'cooling off period' so crimes would not be committed in the heat of controversy. Just a few months later Oregon repealed the waiting period. Nowadays, you don't need a permit, license, or registration to obtain a gun immediately in Oregon. There isn't even a state Child Access Prevention Law that requires adults to store guns out of the reach of minors.

"Can't do that my friend. You can buy it now, but pick up will be in five days," he said.

I pulled out a large stack of twenty-dollar bills and laid it on the counter.

"How much is there?" Harley-Man asked.

"Five hundred dollars."

He walked over to the front door and changed the sign to 'CLOSED FOR BUSINESS'. It was 6 p.m. anyway and nobody else was in his shop. There was one window, and he drew down the shade.

"Strip to your underwear," he commanded. My thoughts flashed to the scene in Pulp Fiction when Bruce Willis and Ving Rhames met the Gimp in the pawnshop basement.

"Excuse me?"

"You heard me, boy. You want a gun? Then you strip."

It was obvious he meant business, but it was not obvious how the rest of the business would be conducted. If he wanted to rape me he could just hold me at gunpoint and do it. Perhaps it wasn't a great instinct, but for some reason I trusted him. He took my clothes and searched every inch with his filthy callused hands. I noticed his bicep tattoo stated:

SURGEON GENERAL WARNING:
Harassing me about drinking is hazardous to your health

"Just making sure you're not wired," he explained.

After taking my wallet out of my pants, he went through every credit card and billfold. He saw I carried a lot more cash. Harley-Man found my state doctors license, malpractice insurance card, and American Medical Association Visa card.

"Doctor huh? Just had to make sure you weren't a cop. Get dressed." He threw my clothes back at me. I felt a physical wave of relief, but was embarrassed to be standing in my tighty whities, just praying there wasn't a brown stain on the back of them. I really need to get some boxer shorts. Jewish guys with back hair just don't look good in white undies.

Harley-Man took me into a back room. He opened a metal file cabinet with a key. There were four handguns in it.

"These are all unregistered, unmarked, untraceable guns my friend. The cheapest of 'em is this here Smith & Wesson for $800. The Ruger P90 is $950, and the Beretta 9mm is $1200. This here Glock 35

Tactical is $1500 and it is guaranteed to finish any job. It is accurate and high caliber. It does not miss."

I didn't have near that kind of money on me.

"$1500? Are you kidding me? I can remove an appendix for half that price."

He didn't see the humor in my joke.

"Hey man, this is non-negotiable. You either need the job done right or you don't. Let's wrap this up."

I definitely didn't need the best. The idea of the Glock was exciting. The Smith & Wesson made more sense. If I actually had to shoot Earl, I really didn't want to kill him. A simple disabling wound would be easier for me to deal with.

"I'll take the Smith & Wesson." There was $260 in my wallet, in addition to the $500 in twenties already in front of him.

Harley-Man took the $760 and told me I owed him $40 and a favor.

He asked, "Anything else, Doc? Ammunition, stun gun, handcuffs, duct tape?"

"You know I don't have any more money on me."

"You got a credit card, Doc. Those things are all completely legal, my friend."

A stun gun sounded more appealing than shooting Earl. It hadn't dawned on me to just use a stun gun. I was tempted to ask if I could cancel the Smith & Wesson purchase and just get the stun gun. One look at Harley-Man and I sensed that request wouldn't go over well. So, I purchased the Smith & Wesson, stun gun, bullets, handcuffs, and of course duct tape.

The longer I live here, the more I realize that too many Portlanders presume that everything is legal as long as you don't get caught. It's been that way ever since the late 1800s, when a clever law-skirting entrepreneur, Sweet Mary, arrived in town. Mary set up a floating brothel on a barge that cruised up and down the Willamette River. Her whore house was not technically within city limits, so she didn't have to worry about city laws, and she never had to pay city taxes. Whether it is Sweet Mary or Big Bob's Pawnshop, it just goes to show that Roman playwright Lucius Seneca was correct when he philosophized that *laws don't persuade just because they threaten.*

SIXTEEN

I was feeling a little guilty not telling Karen about the gun, but decided there was no way she would have acquiesced to my purchase. She wouldn't understand the critical importance of the current situation, or how I planned to handle it. Usually her instincts are right, but not always. I learned that lesson on one of our first dates.

Several years ago we were traveling on a rural road when a car in front of us hit a deer. The deer lay injured on the side of the road, obviously in great distress. Karen, also in distress about the situation, actually pulled the deer into her lap and began comforting it. The deer struggled initially, but eventually relaxed in her grasp. Holding the deer with her right arm, Karen called her veterinarian with the phone in her left hand.

The police arrived and urged her to let go of the deer, but she refused.

"Ma'am, please let go of the deer."

"It's injured. I have to keep comforting it."

The cop repeated, "Ma'am, let go of the deer now, and move away from the scene."

Karen sharply replied, "What is wrong with you! Can't you see this animal is injured? It may have a broken spinal cord! We need to keep it still."

"If you don't let go of the deer, I will have you arrested. Let go of the deer now."

Karen was afraid of what the cop would do to the deer, not to her. She knew it was police policy to shoot a suffering animal hit by a car. I asked the cop to give me a minute to talk with her so that I could try to convince Karen that it would be best for her and the animal to let the officer do his job. She had a look of defeat on her face, yet finally obliged.

When she released the deer, it stood up, and then swiftly pranced into the woods without the slightest limp. The deer wasn't fatally injured; it just had the wind knocked out of it. Karen got the prognosis wrong, just as doctors sometimes do.

This incident reminded me that there are always exceptions to the rule, and helped me justify my gun purchase. Do guns regularly kill innocent people and loved ones? Yes. Do most deer hit on the side of the road end up fatally injured? Yes. Would Earl resort to violence?

My phone started vibrating in my pocket as I drove the slick roads towards Earl's house. The caller I.D. indicated it was Grant.

"Grant, what's going on?"

"Listen Jerry, I didn't want to bog you down with all of my personal crap, but I also don't want you to feel like you're out of the loop."

"Grant, I shouldn't have asked you about your marriage intentions. That stuff was between you and Tarini. You didn't have to share it with me. The fact that you did, is in a way, well, an honor. Really. You were one of the first people to befriend me when I moved out here. You'll always be a great friend, and I want you to feel like you can tell me that kind of stuff. Likewise, if you're uncomfortable about discussing something, wait till the time is right."

"I appreciate that, because there are a few more things I'd like to share with you."

"What's that? Anything you need to tell me, just get it off your chest."

The damn cell phone was breaking up slightly after every few words, and the conversation did not feel as genuine or as intense as it did at his house. I wanted to hear what Grant had to say. He was going through a period of hell. Heedful of those issues, I turned my car onto a narrow street and pulled to a stop on the side of the road. My full attention was now his.

He explained, "You know, I met Tarini just after her baby aspirated on its emesis."

"I didn't know that. It must have been tough meeting her just after her baby died."

"Well, her baby wasn't dead."

"What do you mean? You said it was found blue."

"That *is* what I said. But the baby began breathing again after she cleared its airway and gave it mouth-to-mouth. The baby lived another nine days on a ventilator. The child was in a terrible predicament. Tarini knew it was time to allow it to die. She made the right choice, as she always did."

"Wow, Grant. That must have been terrible. It adds another dimension to who she was. Now I understand why Tarini always seemed like she had wisdom and experience beyond her years."

"You know, at the time, I was in medical school at Oregon Health Sciences University. My rotation in pediatrics had only a week remaining when her baby was admitted to critical care. Obviously, as a medical student I didn't have much responsibility with the care of a really sick baby. I just watched that child slowly decline and take a little piece of Tarini with it every day. There wasn't much of an age difference between Tarini and myself. I think we all empathize a little more with people we relate to. My thoughts of how dreadful the whole ordeal must be for her consumed me. Every chance I could, I would go and hang out with her in the mournful waiting room.

"We had an unusual connection even then. Not love, but understanding. We had some of the deepest conversations about life and suffering. I always felt a little guilty around her. Both then, and even now when she's not here. I'm aware I never actually did anything to feel guilty about. It's kind of like the way white people sometimes feel guilty for slavery and racism when we are around black people. Even though you know it's something you were never involved in, it can somehow make you feel repentant. People can go through some terrible stuff. I guess we sometimes experience remorse since we are part of the human race, and in some way feel we share in the blame indirectly."

"Were you there when the ventilator was withdrawn?" I asked as delicately as I could manage.

"No. That happened two days after my pediatrics rotation was done. Her child was in critical care at Legacy Emmanuel Hospital. I had just started my rotation in cardiology across town at Veterans Hospital when I got the news she had decided to withdraw care. I really wish… I really wish I had been there to support her that day. You can imagine."

"Did you guys stay friends ever since that time?" I gently asked.

"Not really. I did call her to offer my condolences. We talked for a while on the phone. I didn't see her for several years. One day, when I was a senior resident at OHSU, we ran into each other again.

This time she was wearing a medical student's white jacket. It was awkward the first few seconds, but we soon felt really comfortable around each other again."

"Once more, thanks for sharing that with me. It gives me a better appreciation of Tarini *and* you."

"Listen, Jerry, it's not really why I called, but it does feel better talking about this stuff. The last few days, all these emotions have been driving me crazy. There is more I need to discuss with you. Can you come on over?"

How many times in life have we all said the following to someone going through a rough patch, *'If there is anything I can do, just call me. Seriously, anything'*? We all know there is usually nothing we can do. We all know that person will never call us asking for a favor. Yet, we say it anyway to make us feel better that we offered. At that moment, one of my best friends was reaching out for help in a time of need. He made the call. Anyone would have dropped everything and headed straight for his house.

I whispered in true frustration, "Oh, man."

Then in a louder but still frustrated voice said, "You'll understand why later, but I can't come over right now."

"Why, what are you doing?"

"I promise to tell you later, Grant. It's just really important. Believe me, as soon as I get done with this, I'm coming over. It might take a little while, but I'll be there. I promise."

SEVENTEEN

I once witnessed a surgeon faint while watching his three-year old son get stitches in the emergency room. Another reminder that situations which never bothered you professionally can become unbearable when personalized. On my way to settling with Earl, I prayed for the composure so many movie heroes exhibit on screen. I tuned into Portland's college radio KPSU 98.3 FM, itching to hear a soothing song. The song was 'Living on Earth' by a local lesbian band called Mommy Ate Your Daddy:

> Fault lines separate land,
> creating cultures, to misunderstand.
> Yeah, yeah, yeah, I don't give a crap.
> Insects in the field chirp loudly,
> blocking panicked thoughts within.
> Hurtful sorrow and fears,
> blend to form religions.
> Big values, should have no price,
> just nobody agrees what they are.
> Yeah, yeah, yeah, who gives a crap?

The blinding glare created by the setting sun on the wet asphalt made driving difficult and encouraged me to stop for a single malt scotch. A drink would ease my anxiety, I convinced myself. In Multnomah Village, a Portland suburb consisting of a few unique blocks filled with antique stores, there was a low-key bar called The Ship. I grabbed the twenty dollars I always kept in my glove compartment for 'just-in-case' scenarios.

"Give me the best whiskey on the rocks this will buy me," I said, dropping the twenty on the bar. The bartender gave me a generous pour of Aberlour Single Highland Malt that had been aged 21 years, and took the entire twenty. There was dust on the bottle, but the scotch had a smooth aftertaste with hints of vanilla and smokiness.

The Other Face Of Murder

The Scottish pride in their handcrafted whiskeys is well deserved. A Scottish friend once told me, *Scotland is a place where Jesus could never have been born. You could never find three wise men or a virgin there, but goddamn if we don't make great whiskey.*

I got back on the road, drove to a forest preserve near Earl's house, and then sat in my red Subaru planning my confrontation with Earl. The sun had set. Earlier there had been a cloudburst, but the precipitation had returned to the usual fine northwestern drizzle. The moist air soothed my dry throat. I spotted a Northern Pygmy Owl - a small brown owl decorated with plentiful small white dots - perched atop one of the smaller Douglas-fir trees at the edge of the forest preserve. Its body was still except for its tail -- twitching, as if trying to tell me that my ass looked scared. Pygmy owls used to be thought of as very secretive birds, but recently they adapted by learning to hunt in the numerous man-made forest clearings. While major steps in evolution can take thousands of years, several species have evolved more quickly to confront the rapid changes in their environment, just as the Northern Pygmy Owl did. Adapting and evolving are necessary survival skills for all species. Bacteria develop resistance mechanisms everyday to our modern antibiotics as proof that microevolution within species occurs at rapid rates. That's why we scientists know it's no longer correct to call evolution *a theory*. Be that as it may, I wasn't optimistic I could evolve from a skinny Jewish doctor to Superman within minutes.

It seemed best to walk a quarter mile down the street rather than park in Earl's driveway. That way, I foolishly reasoned, if something happened there wouldn't be any witnesses. I was wearing a fuzzy blue fleece jacket from L.L. Bean with pockets big enough to manage the gun, handcuffs, stun gun, and duct tape. I hoped Earl wouldn't notice the unusual bulges.

Instead of knocking, I went around to his back porch. Earl lives in a historic section of town. His dwelling was more like a charming old-fashioned cottage than a house. The painted white wood floor of the deck creaked slightly and I worried he would hear me. Fortunately, the sound of rain water dropping on the partially rusted gutters was louder than my steps.

Earl's friends knew he kept a key to his back door under an

empty ceramic flowerpot next to the doormat. His new doormat reminded guests to 'WIPE YOUR PAWS'. Earl does not even like dogs. Most likely he purchased the mat because it was on sale. Bargains always surpassed style when it came to his clothes or home decorating.

I was able to open the screen door and unlock the back door without making much noise, and found myself in his mud room amid several pairs of dirt-caked sneakers that were strewn about. Darkness predominated, but some light came from an outside yard lamp. I resisted pulling the string of a single 60-watt light bulb that hung from the ceiling. The intention wasn't to ambush Earl, but I wanted the element of surprise working in my favor. If he was a murderer, knocking on the front door would allow him time to arm himself before answering the door.

My heart palpitated so strongly against my ribs that the pulsations were plainly audible to my ears. CNN blared from the front room. Some clanking and sizzling sounds seemed to be coming from the kitchen. The slight shiver in my hands migrated to my lower lip. I slowly moved through the arched hallway that connected the mud room to the kitchen, then stopped cold. I couldn't have come across a more ominous scene. Earl was slicing meat on his cutting board. The raw flesh was bloody and the juices were dripping off the cutting board onto the bright yellow tile counter. He had neglected to roll up the cuffs of his clay colored flannel shirt, so both cuffs exhibited blood stains. Hearing or sensing my presence, he turned around with a look of alarm and had the large carving knife still in his grasp.

"In the name of Christ, Jerry! What gives?"

"You didn't answer the front door. I guess the TV was too loud."

"So you couldn't knock on the back door? You just barge in here? You scared me half to death man."

He had a point. I clutched the Smith & Wesson hidden in my pocket. The safety was off.

"What's going on with the Phil Michaelson case?" I asked.

"Well butter my ass and call me a biscuit. First of all Jerry, you barge into my house unexpected and uninvited. Now, in a very accusatory manner you bring up a painful experience, which by the way you are getting too good at doing. You should have been a lawyer, not a doctor. What axe are you trying to grind? Most important, you have no right to know anything about that case. It is a private matter between me, the Michaelson family, and the half-witted lawyers involved. You keep this up and I'll put my foot so far up your ass that your breath will smell like shoe polish."

He certainly wasn't trying to disguise his agitation. My next accusation was not about to lessen his anger.

"I know who the primary care doctor was that screwed you. You could have…"

"Oh fuck you! Fuck you!!"

He squared his broad shoulders and started walking towards me in an intimidating manner. Almost unconsciously I pulled my gun into full view. Earl stepped back startled, bumping his lower back against the kitchen counter. He placed the knife down on the cutting board.

"So, are you going to shoot me now? Is that what you came here to do? You stupid bastard. You have no idea what you're doing, do you?"

He inched his way towards me. I unloaded a round in his right leg. He dropped to the ground screaming. I couldn't believe I actually shot him. Sometimes there is something inside yourself that you never knew you had. Trapped ingredients revealed only during turmoil. Unthinkable deeds, such as shooting a friend, go a long way towards proving that in the end humans are all just glorified monkeys. At that moment, I came to grips with the uneasy feeling that I had previously refused to face. Achieving justice wasn't my predominant motivation. It was about revenge. Revenge both for Tarini, and for soiling the sacredness of my home. No longer was it about apprehending the guy that did this, but it was more about making him pay.

"You fucking moron! Damn that hurts! Oh, my God! Fuck!" Earl was squirming in pain. Blood streaked across the kitchen floor with every movement of his leg. With a tumultuous delivery he admonished me.

"You know what ties together people like Bin Laden and Jerry Falwell and Jerry Weissman? It's that they are certain they are correct. That even death is justifiable to achieve the direction they want to see the world take. They never doubt that their opinions are irrefutable and infallible. That's what makes them fanatics. That's what makes you a son-of-a-bitch fanatic!"

"You killed Tarini, didn't you, Earl?" The way I vocalized the question was eerie even to me. The query was asked without panic, slowly and calmly, which was not at all how I felt inside.

"Just give it a rest, would you? Even the smartest person in the world doesn't know much about most things!"

Earl's leg was bleeding profusely, but not fast enough for him to die of blood loss. There were mild pulsations of dark red that indicated I had hit the venous system and not the high pressure bright red arterial vessels. Either from the hurt or fear, he vomited. He grabbed a dishcloth hanging from the cabinet next to him. In agony, he tied the cloth around the wound on his leg to control the bleeding.

Earl turned to me and asked, "Now what?"

Good question. What were we to do? Calling the cops was out of the question, because I first needed him to confess to the murder. Getting that closure was important to me emotionally. Also, I needed him to give me details that only the killer would know, evidence that might have gotten me out of trouble for undertaking violent action against him. Killing him was definitely not my intention. I fumbled for the stun gun in my other pocket. When I pulled it out, he gave me a look of consternation. He could read the intimidating inscription on the device, 'Z-FORCE 100,000V'.

"Time to level with me," I told him.

After staring at the 'Z-FORCE 100,000V', he looked directly into my eyes. I was kneeling only a few feet away from him. He then appeared to be looking above and behind me. It wasn't a trick I was going to fall for. Everyone knows how that works. I would turn around and then he'd attack me. Well, in retrospect I guess I should have turned around. A bolt of thunder went off in the back of my head. The room hazed over and a sheet of black veiled my vision. In a dreamy state, I concentrated on begging my body not to wilt, but my muscles wouldn't follow orders. The most curious aspect that I recall about the experience was how much we can think about the past, present, and future in such a short period of time. Thoughts raced through my head about death, of how Karen and my mother would each face my absence, and about who might have done this to me. As I fell, I desperately tried to recognize the muffled voice behind me. Those emotions changed to inconsolable disappointment with the thud of my head striking the floor. Wisdom derived from mistakes occasionally lacks benefit. Sometimes we will never encounter a similar dilemma again. My final thought, as I lost consciousness, was that I had let Tarini down – again.

EIGHTEEN

I'm not sure exactly how long it took to regain consciousness, but likely, it was no more than a few minutes. When I did recover my senses, I tried to move and found my ability to do so was limited. The handcuffs I had purchased from Harley-Man to use on Earl were now securely on me. My frozen wrists were connected to a wall pipe in a dark cellar; yet I was still thankful I was not attached to the scalding hot water pipe my shin briefly touched as I attempted to change positions. A dank smell of humid cardboard was lingering around my nose and mouth. I looked around and saw stacks of cardboard boxes surrounding me. My aching head craved Tylenol, and I was unsure of my whereabouts. My recollection of those hours is rather limited. I was aware of my exhaustion, and despite my cramped and uncomfortable position, sleep soon overcame me. When I next opened my eyes, I could tell from the light coming through a cubbyhole of a window above my head, that the night had passed and morning had arrived. Sometimes the seemingly best plans bring out the worst surprises, I thought to myself. That depressing reflection brought Paul to mind, a guy I chatted up in 1992 at a coffee shop in California.

My hospitalized patients have often recounted how they became obsessively focused on an absurd topic while under stress. Oftentimes, it will be a silly song or event they can't get out of their head. In my case, uninvited flashbacks of Paul afflicted my already jumbled cognition during my captivity. In Hollywood, it isn't unusual to meet people who have had sex changes. Paul used to be a butch-dressed woman, and still wore his customary black leather jacket and faded Levi blue jeans. What was unusual was Paul's candor. It's not often you find a transgender person willing to open up to a stranger about the most intimate details.

Out of genuine interest, I asked him what he had found to be the most unexpected aspect of becoming a man. He hadn't been surprised by negative reactions from family, friends, and coworkers, he declared. What shocked him, and fascinated me, were the cerebral effects of the supra-therapeutic dosages of testosterone he took to maintain his new male physical features. These weren't the prescribed doses a middle-aged man low on his testosterone level gets from his doctor to maintain libido. Paul had injected the kind of monstrous dosages weight lifters take illegally.

Even though Paul, as a woman, had shunned femininity and had adopted male fashion, she nevertheless had loathed the stereotypical male obsession with sex and other testosterone-driven behaviors, such as our fascination with contact sports, guns, and violence.

The testosterone factor may be the reason why boys typically are not as emotionally mature as girls. Once testosterone levels rise, boys can't concentrate on anything beyond sex. They'll sit in their high school classes without hearing a word the teacher says, just looking at all the girls and wondering what it would take to shag them. Even the fat chicks enter their perverted thoughts.

That was Paul's surprise. During his first visit to an athletic club shortly after his first hormone injection, his mind became consumed with sex. At that moment, he realized he would have said anything to any of those lovely young women, no matter how big the lie, if it would get him what he wanted. He had become one of us. Testosterone changes physical features, but it has even more powerful effects on the psyche. It was an unwelcome surprise Paul couldn't have predicted.

Like Paul, I had a few unwelcome realities to confront. The ambush I planned had backfired badly. Perhaps too much testosterone was traveling through me, because I felt enraged. It crossed my mind that I probably understood Paul, after an hour's conversation, much better than I knew Earl, despite him being my best friend for years. The natural reaction was to try to escape, but the handcuffs clanking against the metal pipe only alerted my captors. The television blaring through the ceiling was abruptly turned off. Someone was making his way down the ratchety stairs to the basement where my weakened body was confined.

Each time a stair creaked, "fuuuuck," would simultaneously be emitted from a muffled voice.

A paroxysm of fear surged through me. Rage instantaneously

morphed into anxiety and timidity. That was the most helpless I'd ever felt. Some tears rolled down my cheeks, but I remained silent while making a pathetic attempt to suppress my emotions by thinking about baseball. Nobody wants to appear cowardly in front of a captor. I sucked and swallowed the thick dripping snot accumulating on my upper lip. The room must have been used for the storage of valuables because someone was unlocking a padlocked door.

Earl's noxious gaze made me wish he'd refrain from uttering whatever statement was about to exit his mouth. "Look at you all hog tied now. Do you have any idea how painful it is to go down a flight of stairs after you've been shot in the leg? Ughhh! You stupid fucking asshole. Did I miss out on something here? Was yesterday 'shoot your best friend day' or something?"

There was another set of feet clunking down the stairs. Meanwhile, Earl limped towards me, and then sat down beside me. He clutched his calf where a white gauze bandage was wrapped around the bullet wound. Most of his fingernails were short from his nail-biting habit. The few nails of normal length revealed dried blood beneath them from tending his wound. Earl's pitch black pupils beamed at me with hostility. Then for the first and last time in our relationship, he recited some original poetry.

> The sun toys with the planet,
> Energizing the game called life.
> Like I should toy with your liver,
> With my guthook hunting knife.

His notably awkward manners were always compensated by unparalleled wit. The words continued to sink in for a few moments. Earl unlocked the handcuffs. He seemed let down that I didn't verbally acknowledge his proficiency with the English language.

"Come on, Jerry, you have no response to that? I wrote it just for you. Perhaps it's not Dickinson or Blake, but I'm only an amateur. Anyhow, don't take all the words literally. Words and thoughts get so twisted. Just because somebody says something, doesn't mean it will come true. You're all bent out of shape because you haven't learned to be flexible.

NINETEEN

The shadowy figure standing behind Earl was unmistakable.

"Hi Jerry. Sorry about the blow to the head," Grant said with sincerity. He handed me a glass of water, which I drank.

Earl interjected, "Oh yeah, really sorry. This is really great hanging out with you two today. The fresh leg wound is a particular bonus. If things get any better, I may seriously need to hire somebody to help me enjoy it. I was supposed to be golfing right now, but when the opportunity to be with my good friends came calling, how could I turn that there down?"

In hindsight I've reflected about all the dignified responses I could have said in reply to Earl. Instead, I responded with cynicism, "Good for you, Earl. Golf is for people who don't like their families."

"What?"

"It's a game for people who don't like their families," I repeated, enunciating each word. "You play it on your day off. Eighteen holes on the day you should be with your family. Values. It's a value thing. Something you need to learn a little about."

Those were the last words I said for a while. A closed fist slammed into my upper abdomen. The bitter taste in my mouth and a burning esophagus were only the beginning of an almost unbearable discomfort. The next sensation of not getting any air was accompanied by intense nausea and vomiting. The glass of water in my stomach emptied on my shirt incompletely mixed with bile and stomach acid. A tea kettle eerily started to shrill in the background, which I prayed Earl would attend to, but he ignored it.

"Oh, I'm sorry Jerry, were you sayin' something? Can you repeat that please? My nervous tic disorder just got a little out of hand. Perhaps I'm a little upset about something. I'm trying to give a shit about your point of view, and when that happens, you'll be the first to know," Earl stated, sounding perturbed.

Then he put his mouth an inch from my ear and yelled, "Did it ever occur to you that I don't have any goddamn family here in

Portland? I left my forebears so I could have a good time out here. As a family man, my affection for my kin is unquestionable, as long as I can live in a city more than a stone's throw away from them. If I wanted to hang out with my redneck family to enjoy weekend sports like cow tipping, I'd return to Alabama. If I want to golf, I'll fucking go golfing!"

The spit he showered on my face didn't concern me as much as my powerlessness to inhale. A squeezing in my abdomen and chest prohibited air from entering through my gasping lips. While the pain was severe, the thought of crying out was ridiculous since it would waste the few precious molecules of oxygen I was clinging to. Of all the cravings a person can have, none will ever be as intense as the yearning for air.

I ran my free hand through my hair. It felt sticky and contained some crusts of hardened blood.

Earl completed his commentary. "Of course, the ability to walk down the fairway again would be nice. Eh, who cares, right? Like I need another rainy golf day. Go wash up. We got things to discuss."

At times, Karen has accused me of spending too much time with Earl. She's always been amused by him, but there's something about him she's never fully trusted. She told me, *Earl's like a mountain lion. You want to witness his magnificence, but not from too close a distance.* Having entered the lion's den, Karen's wariness regarding Earl started to make perfect sense.

Earl went back upstairs, screaming the occasional curse whenever he put weight on his right leg. The soreness in my abdomen and a dizzying headache allowed me to empathize with piñatas.

Grant stayed with me until I could walk, and eventually helped me upstairs to a bathroom. Many bathrooms in moist environments have mold problems. The brown fern-patterned mold was creeping through the small cracks of the white plastered walls. Like all the other bathrooms in Earl's house, there was a collection of soaps, shampoos, and mouthwash on the sink counter. Not the designer soaps one finds in upscale fragrance and soap boutiques. Not the cute little bathroom soaps you get as gifts. These were from Earl's hotel and motel collection. He even kept those stupid shower caps they leave in the bathrooms. He's never used a shower cap. Rarely does Earl get lucky enough to have an overnight guest. When he does, will anyone ever be eager to take a shower with a tiny plastic shower cap? Why even take a shower if you're not planning to wash your hair? You might as well just pull out the deodorant stick and apply another layer until you have time for a genuine cleaning.

    Looking at my stubble-covered face in the mirror was surreal. The truth a mirror reveals can be sadistic. Puke on my shirt. My hair was sticky, bloody, greasy and disheveled. Sweaty armpits, unchanged underwear, soggy socks, and unbrushed teeth complemented the pungent odor of vomit. Disgusting, like a porous condom that limits pleasure yet allows exposure to sleaze. That's how I felt, and was, on the inside and out. I reasoned that the future was important, and the past would speak for itself soon enough; that what's inside is always what matters most. Unfortunately, the answer of who exactly I was remained uncertain to me. When one learns that friendships aren't what they appeared to be, one also learns that you are not who you think you are.

TWENTY

After washing up, and regaining the ability to breath and talk, I wobbled into the living room. They weren't there. It occurred to me that I could just run out the front door. Charging outside into the northwestern rain could conceivably wipe away the accumulated filth and simultaneously save my life. That being said, if they had wanted to kill me, they would have already done so. Also, my trembling legs barely kept me walking, let alone running. I sat on Earl's couch and tried to come up with a strategy.

A good musician needs more than talent and skill. A musician must be persuasive. Members of an audience bring their own baggage to the concert. Maybe they are in a good mood, or maybe they had a really bad day. Perhaps a concertgoer just had an argument with a spouse, or a loss in the stock market. Whatever the situation, the musician must sway the audience to have a good experience.

A doctor's patients are even more of a challenge than a musician's audience. The patient is always having a bad time. That's why they are paying to see you. A good doctor needs more than skills and talent. Even with the best drugs, the patient may leave the office with fatigue or discomfort. A doctor must change thinking and attitudes to instill a sense of hope and well-being, even though reality may be unpleasant. Sometimes, we inoculate the patient with bullshit. Earl, Grant, and I were all masters of dealing with unpleasant reality. We could dish out the bullshit as well as anyone. The three of us were all trained and disciplined in the art of logical debate, scientific defense, and questioning. Fortunately, we were also trained in diagnosing and solving problems with diplomatic attentiveness. A skilled battle of wits was about to transpire, but words weren't flowing easily through my battered brain. They had the upper hand.

Earl hobbled into the room holding a McTarnahans Ale that kept spilling each time he put weight on his listless leg. Any good clinician knows to start with open-ended questions. And that is exactly what Earl did in his own sarcastic way.

"So my ornery little friend, something on your noggin?"

Grant entered the room also with a beer in hand.

I really wanted to respond with, 'No, my friend, is something in your leg?', but I chose to avoid having the air knocked out of me again.

Incomprehensible deception among friends infected the atmosphere. Getting to the truth was my sole desire.

"Guys, I know how Tarini died."

Earl's piercing response caught me off guard. "Let me guess. She got a shot of Vecuronium up the ass?"

To which I acknowledged, "God, that is just an amazing guess. You must be frickin' psychic, because that's exactly what happened."

The most disturbing thing was not that Earl had killed her. His role in the murder had already started to sink in. How and why Grant was involved, was beyond me. He always seemed to show Tarini devoted love. My insides felt hollow with anger, and I suspected much of my energy, in the future, would be spent on re-centering my soul.

Grant seemed distant and guarded. "We didn't kill her. We helped her die."

"Oh, I know. I wasn't going to accuse you guys of killing her. Obviously, she wanted you to inject her with a paralyzing agent up her ass. Isn't that what everyone wants these days?"

"She did," said Grant, without sarcasm. But I kept the sarcasm game going.

"Oh ... Well, there you go. How stupid of me to think otherwise. I'll tell you what. Let's just chalk all this up to a big misunderstanding. As long as nobody carries any hurt feelings, we can leave things just as they were before Tarini died."

Earl jumped in, "Well tickle my balls, he doesn't believe us, Grant."

They each gave me the serious look. That look signifies the moment when scam artists pull out everything they have. They glanced at each other, and Earl gave Grant a gesture that indicated Grant should be the one to spin the story.

"Tarini had four major seizures. Eventually she got an MRI. It conclusively showed a glioblastoma beyond surgical resection." Grant took a few moments to compose himself, then solemnly forged ahead.

"We figured it would be found at autopsy and that would be the end of it. Obviously, when her family rejected a face and brain autopsy, our plan got messed up."

A glioblastoma is a fatal brain cancer. They can grow at a tragic rate, and generally are completely unresponsive to chemotherapy. In the uncommon event of an early diagnosis, surgical removal can be attempted. Even with a surgical cure, there will often be serious brain damage because the chunk of brain the tumor infiltrates must also be removed. Almost always, the diagnosis is made at stages beyond surgical cure. Grant was also right about the family refusing a brain autopsy. Families frequently will allow exploration of all parts of the body with the exception of the brain. Giving consent to cutting through a person's skull into the most vital structure of the personality is not easy for anyone. Families also worry about an open-casket. They can't envision their loved one looking the same after a saw cuts through the cranium, even though the pathologist sews the skull cap together in a precise manner that allows for unhindered viewing of the body.

I had to admit they came up with a great story. Not that it much changed my opinion of their actions. All three of us had taken the oath to *first do no harm,* as well as an oath to *not administer poison to anyone when asked.* We're healers, not killers. While it was fine with me to withdraw life support in a terminally ill patient, the notion of purposefully speeding up Tarini's fate sounded unjustifiable. My father had committed suicide, and it was tragic enough that he undertook that action on his own. If others had helped him die, my bitterness would be even stronger.

Their story made me pause for a moment. "Did you ever consider trying to inspire hope in Tarini instead of just exterminating her?"

Earl stroked his eyebrow, and countered with, "Hey, we know as well as anyone that attitude influences physical health. We tried to convince her to fight this thing until the end. Her opinions were firm about what she wanted. Here's the thing, it wasn't about any of us folks. It was about her. Loyalty towards friends is something you lack. Maybe that's why she didn't tell you about it."

That really got under my bones. The conceited suggestion that out of the three of us, I was the un-loyal friend, made me want to exterminate Earl.

They waited patiently for my retort.

"I don't believe any of it for a second. She didn't have cancer! There's something more to all this. You both have good paying careers, so it can't be about money. What was the motive?"

They wouldn't verbally respond, but reciprocated in sighs and groans.

"Well," I said, "let's just go down to the hospital and check the MRI films. It's as simple as that."

"I wish it were, Jerry," said Grant. "We wish we had the films on us right now to show you. Tarini checked out the films. She sent them to her radiologist friend at the Mayo Clinic for a second opinion, which he grimly gave her. He is sending the films back to the hospital. They will be here in a few days. You can look at them then."

"I don't have a few days. This has to be solved by nine tomorrow morning or the police will be called. It's out of my control."

"Who is fixin' to call the police?" asked Earl.

There was no way I was going to give up Dr. Klaus Vanwaggen. As much of a pain in the ass as he was, he didn't deserve to die over this.

"So now the truth comes out. You need to know who has knowledge of the case. You have to take care of those loose ends, don't you?"

Earl was pissed, "You are just one stupid dipweed, aren't you? This wouldn't even be an issue if you had just left well enough alone. First you shoot me, and now the potential for cops getting involved exists. Lately, being around you has been more depressing than being around a patient with end-stage eye cancer. What's next, Jerry? What do you have left in you?"

"Listen, you two are the assholes. Even if she did have a glioblastoma, she died a bad death. Suffocating in a closet? Give me a break!"

"O.K." said Grant. "Let's not even go there for now. You need to be proven one piece of the pie at a time. None of us are brain surgeons, and we are not going to cut into her head in an amateurish manner this afternoon. I can't even tolerate seeing her dead. Believe it or not, Jerry, I'm hurting more than you can imagine right now. I lost the love of my life. You two need to go down to the hospital and MRI her brain to obtain the images that prove her cancer exists."

"What?" screamed Earl. "I hate to sound rude, but maybe you're forgetting she is a corpse. A corpse doesn't get an MRI. They get autopsies. Both of you are going off the deep end on this one. You're simply way off base. Just because a chicken has wings, it don't mean it can fly. Looks can be deceiving, my friend. The last thing we all need is more crazy schemes to get us into trouble. Anyway, how are we going to convince a radiologist and radiology tech to do an MRI at the last minute on a deceased body?"

"We can get it done," I said with some hesitation. The avenues of my life continue to lead me back to the damn hospital. Whether it's personal, professional, or the blurring line in every doctor's life, it always seems to pull me back to the hospital. Modern society reveres hospitals, but I regard them as shrines to the feeble and infirm. However, I did need the truth, and the hospital was the only place to discover it. "MRI closes at 5 p.m. We can do it after closing time. Earl, you call your radiology technician friend to fire up the MRI machine. We don't need a radiologist involved. If her tumor is that big, I can interpret the films myself."

Earl replied, "The day is still plenty early. We might as well continue to look for as much trouble as we can. Why stop now? No reason to piddle around here all day."

TWENTY-ONE

We had to kill three or four hours so that we would arrive at MRI well after 5 p.m. Earl used that time to treat his leg wound, while I tried to recover further from the blow to my head. I was still feeling a certain degree of nausea.

Earl let me borrow a navy blue sweatshirt that was a few sizes too big. Since he was having so much pain walking, I became his chauffer. Still achy from being punched in the stomach and hit on the head, I sluggishly retrieved my car from the lot in the forest preserve and pulled into his driveway. He slowly got in. My head still teetered like a seesaw. Getting behind the wheel after a tequila tasting party would have been safer than me driving at that moment.

"How's your leg?" I asked, while eyeballing the nearly empty gas gauge.

"The bullet went through my calf muscle. Lucky that you're a lousy shot. It missed the bone. This wound should heal in a few weeks."

"Listen, Tarini is locked up in the pathology department. We'll need to stop by Klaus Vanwaggen's home to get the key."

Earl looked at me in disbelief. "Come on, Jerry, you got that ogre involved?! That's just great. That guy is so unfriendly, they say his own dog don't like him. Sometimes you haven't got the sense God gave a grasshopper."

"County forensics denied the case. He was assigned the case. Believe me, I'd rather he weren't involved right now."

I had not wanted to give that information up. But there was no other option. We really did need a key to the hospital morgue.

Every second in the car with Earl was mentally agonizing. Shared tragedy can unite people, but trepidation divided us. We were both stuck in a mess, so mistrusting of each other that we could barely talk. Earl seemed more vile and repulsive with every tire rotation. A million internet pop-up ads, a thousand dropped cell phone calls, would have been pleasant events compared to sitting with Earl another minute. Somewhere along the line I must have done something really bad to be in such a rotten karma situation. Nothing in my well-intentioned plans to apprehend Earl had worked out. What I had done to deserve that perplexed me.

As a child, I remember shooting a robin with a pellet gun. My father watched me from the window. When he came outside, he picked up the robin and said, "Well, you got her, all right. What was it that she did to you?"

"Nothing, I guess," was my reply. It upset me that the robin may have been a 'she'. Before firing the gun, it didn't cross my mind that I could create a baby bird Bambi. "Nothing? Were you planning to eat it, son?

"No sir."

The robin lay gracefully in his cupped hands, and he continued the interrogation. "Hmm. Why did you want to take away this creature's life?"

"Don't know, I guess."

"Son?"

"Yes sir."

"Ever hear of karma?"

"No sir."

"You will," is all he said. He buried the robin in the back yard, and the mound of dirt served as a reminder to think about my actions. When we discovered chirping fledglings in an abandoned nest the next morning, it troubled my dad even more than it troubled me. Reflecting back, it's understandable why that event threw him into one of his bouts of depression. My grandmother never made it out of the Warsaw Ghetto, and my grandfather later died at the Treblinka death camp. They had used the last of their money to smuggle my dad out of Poland just prior to the Nazi invasion. Observing a parent die for no logical reason, even if that parent was only a robin, evoked powerful memories for my father. It was a lesson I wouldn't forget.

I learned all about karma when my mother's father was killed in a roofing accident some weeks later. Ever since, I always reflect on what I've done to induce bad predicaments.

The radio was off, and the slow rhythmic tapping of raindrops provided the background soundtrack for our commute. It felt cold in the car, like there was an ice sheet between us. We stopped at a gas station to fill up. As usual, Earl didn't offer to chip in a cent towards the gas or the Tylenol he requested me to purchase for his pain. Cheapskates don't change. Umpteen times a year he will tell a waitress that it's his birthday to finagle a free dessert.

When we got to Vanwaggen's house, Earl wisely chose to stay in the car. Walking up the steps to the house, I became aware of a nasty blister forming on the bottom of my foot. During the process of evolution, why haven't humans formed leather pads or hooves to walk on like most mammals? If evolution hasn't taken place, as many contend, then at least they shouldn't call it 'intelligent design'. Roller blades popping out of our feet on-demand would be an intelligent design.

Klaus answered the front door holding a pipe burning sweet smelling tobacco. He wore green flannel pajamas and didn't seem pleased about the interruption.

"I need the key to the morgue, Klaus."

"Ahh.. I zee... No!"

"Klaus, I just want to MRI her brain. Then we'll put the body back where it belongs."

"Who iss vee?" Spittle flew through his teeth onto my neck and shirt.

"I got Earl Haynes in the car with me. He's going to help me get all this done."

"How are you going to get ze MRI done at ziz time of night?"

"Let us worry about that. We just need the key."

He looked at me inquisitively from head to toe. My flimsy body leaned against the doorpost.

"Wait," Klaus said. He closed the door on me, almost smashing my nose. The sound of the deadbolt bothered me, but he soon returned to unlock the door.

"Vhy not autopzy ze brain?"

"Will you come in tonight to do that, Klaus?"

"No!"

"Will you give me past 9 a.m. before you call the cops?"

"No."

"The keys, Klaus. Just give me the keys."

He reached inside his pajama pocket and gave me two keys. One to get into the morgue itself. The other to unlock the padlock on the fridge storing the body.

    When I got back in the car, Earl was on his cell phone.
    "Who the fuck are you calling?!!" I screamed at him.
    "Shuu-ut up, histrionic boy. I'm checking my messages. Why don't you save the drama for your mama?"
    I tore the phone out of his hand. I worried that he might have informed Grant that Dr. Vanwaggen was in on the case. Perhaps, Grant would come over to take care of that problem while Earl took care of me later. The phone was playing back messages when I put it to my ear. I turned off the phone and put it in my pocket.
    "So now you're stealing my phone? Unbelievable, you're acting like pure varmint."
    "Oy vay, you have chutzpah! You'll get it back."
    "I am impressed that you know how to speak Jewish, but it doesn't make up for acting like a moron," Earl grumbled.
    "You think that I'm a moron? Well, Mr. Genius, maybe you'd like to know there is no such thing as 'speaking Jewish'. There's Hebrew, there's Yiddish, and all the other languages we speak, but there is no speaking Jewish."
    "Fine, Mrs. Sensitive, I'm impressed with your ability to speak Hebrew."
    "Yiddish! *Oy vay* and *chutzpah* are Yiddish."
    "Fine, Mrs. Sensitive, I'm impressed by your *Yiddish*. What does *Yiddish* mean anyway?" Earl asked.
    "It's the language Jews spoke pre-Holocaust in Europe. Yiddish is derived from many old European languages, particularly Old German. In fact, the word Yiddish is derived from the German word *Judisch*, which means Jewish."
    "Well God damn! You just told me there is no such thing as speaking Jewish, but you were speaking Yiddish, which means Jewish. You see, Jerry? You're so confused about everything, and I mean everything, that you don't even understand the words coming out of your mouth."
    My points did seem to be pointless. Perhaps I should rely more on my more primitive instincts and training. Survey the scene and practice safety first. That is what I was taught way back when I was an Emergency Medical Technician ambulance driver.

Your accomplishments will mirror your convictions. That is a good thing only if your convictions are undistorted. It seemed to me that Earl and Grant had sinned based on distorted conviction. Even if Tarini had cancer, which seemed doubtful, they still had no right to speed up the process of her demise. Humans shouldn't play God. Fine, sometimes doctors play God in prolonging life, but it's with genuine, good intention. That's why I've distributed petitions among colleagues advocating the overturning of legalized physician assisted suicide in Oregon. Earl, Grant, Tarini, and even Karen, have always disagreed with me about that issue. It's been my unwavering conviction that the public needs to trust that their doctors have no interest in shortening life.

TWENTY-TWO

On the way to the hospital we took the Burnside Bridge. There are 13 bridges in Portland. That has to be expected in a place where almost eight percent of the city property is water. The Burnside Bridge was built in 1926 and is a bascule drawbridge with a mechanical design similar to that of the Tower Bridge in London. Like most bridges in this city, there is a dedicated bicycle lane that is consistently filled with riders. The popularity of the bicycle in such a soggy city had always fascinated me. No matter what the weather, people ride their bikes everywhere. There was a thin veil of fog covering the bridge that night.

Earl asked me, "What was the concept behind Einstein's Theory of Relativity?"

"Seriously? That was premed. Something about how the universe always is in constant motion and there is no such things as universal coordinates," I responded.

"Right," Earl acknowledged. "Ethics can be equally relative."

"Is that so? Thou shall not murder seems like a pretty solid rule of ethics."

"Tell that to the hungry lion. Would murdering Hitler before the Holocaust have been unethical? My ears are wide open."

When we arrived at the hospital, I helped Earl trudge through the corridors. As he leaned on me in my post-concussive state, it must have looked like Helen Keller assisting the Hunchback of Notre Dame. When we got into the morgue, there were about 60 pull-out refrigerated units in the wall. Each one contained a body, and the same key unlocked the units individually.

"Which one is she in?" inquired Earl with searching eyes.

"Don't know," I answered.

We unlocked each stainless steel encasing separately and inspected the respective stiff, cold bodies. About forty corpses later we found Tarini. Neither Earl nor I had seen her since the pantry killing. We both looked down, and then peered awkwardly at each other.

Earl remarked, "I can't believe we are even doing this horseshit. I'm trying here, Jerry. I'm trying to see things from your point of view, but for some reason I just can't stick my head that far up your ass."

"Sorry for the inconvenience. Nothing like death to ruin a perfectly good evening," I said, in an attempt to break the uneasiness.

Earl picked up on the cue and said, "Death. Do we have to call it that? This world has become politically correct enough to change such a morbid sounding word like death. From now on we shall refer to Tarini as being severely *metabolically challenged*. Just nature's way of telling the body to go on strike and take it easy."

A knock on the morgue door startled us. It was Savannah, the radiology tech we asked to help us with the MRI. She didn't know the details of the situation and didn't seem to want to know. She knew that what we were doing was not exactly kosher. Who knows if performing MRI scans on human remains is illegal without consent of the surviving family? Certainly, it is not an issue that comes up often. An MRI can't hurt or alter the deceased, so it didn't conjure up the feeling of behaving badly.

Savannah was a southern raised tomboy. Like most girls that are tomboys, she eventually turned into an attractive woman. They tend to remain athletic as they get older, resulting in firm and toned bodies. The kind of body that makes geriatric men wish they were a few decades younger, and tempts preachers to lay the bible down. Savannah was no exception. And since tomboys grow up with teasing from the boys, they learn to hold their own against them. That too is an attractive quality. Though her face wasn't as attractive as her physique, by no means did she have a 'butter face'. You know, the everything is hot about her 'but her face' saying. Yet, there's no doubt the stares she gets are mostly for her figure – a build that would make most married men unfaithful if she were to give them the chance. Her sassy southern accent is definitely stronger and sexier than Earl's. There aren't many southerners in Portland. Whenever Savannah and Earl converse, it reminds me of two banjos dueling. Just as African-American schoolchildren will talk 'more urban' to their friends in the schoolyard than they will to their white English teacher, when Earl and Savannah talked, they let the down-home jargon fly.

"Well ain't you a pretty sight for sore eyes tonight, Savannah," barked Earl. Nobody ever accused him of being a romantic. His most recent girlfriend was let down by his attempt at a candlelight dinner when the Pizza Hut driver arrived.

"Hush, puppy dog. Let's get on doing whatever we came to get done."

"Yes ma'am. Can you help me and my friend here, who by the way is wound up tighter than a clock, to move this body to the MRI scanner."

"Hello, Dr. Weissman," she nodded towards me.

"Thanks for doing this, Savannah. Really."

"Much obliged, honey," Savannah remarked. Out of curiosity she unzipped the top of the body bag.

"Father in heaven!! Isn't that Doctor...?"

Earl cut her off. "There's the devil in the details here, Savannah, and we don't have time for details."

He pulled out a wad of cash and gave it to Savannah. Later, he made me reimburse him for the payment he gave her. She stared at the money with crafty eyes, then stuffed it in her black bra. The bra was barely showing at the edges of her well-formed cleavage peeking out of her tight v-neck red T-shirt. That was the end of the discussion. She zipped up the body bag, firmly grasped the edge of the bag, and said, "Let's go, boys."

I'm pretty sure Savannah has fake breasts. It's exceedingly seldom to have a thin and trim body with nature providing voluptuous breasts. Like most guys, I have zero problems with them. In fact, I really think HMOs and Medicaid should cover the cost of augmentation. The public at large benefits from seeing them, and they last a lifetime. They also improve the confidence as well as the manipulative power of women who get them. Studies also show that attractive people earn more. If we give college tax breaks to youngsters to help them prosper, can't we also give tax breaks to those wanting breast implants? Besides, if women have stronger earning power after implantation, they might pay back more to the system in taxes than it cost to fund the implants in the first place.

We put Tarini on a metal autopsy table that had four wheels. We rolled her through the hospital hallways. Earl and I leaned on the table to keep from tumbling to the ground, while Savannah did most of the pushing. She looked at us as if we were downtrodden beggars whose shameful lifestyle created our self-induced, deserved hardships. We took an untraditional route using service elevators to get to MRI. Fortunately, we only passed a janitor mopping the floors, and he paid little attention to us. Savannah unlocked the MRI room and in we went.

TWENTY-THREE

Savannah helped get Tarini onto the MRI table, then wheeled the metal autopsy table out of the room. She went to the control room to start up the computer and software needed to produce the images. Earl and I remained in the MRI scanner room with Tarini. Now that Tarini was out of the frozen morgue, a slight frost precipitated on her dark skin.

Earl was dreaming about Savannah. "She is so damn good looking I would eat her poop if she wanted me to." He is the horniest guy I've ever known. The man had a fresh bullet in his leg, but that didn't temper his libido. If Earl had the chance, he would probably hit on a good looking woman in an STD clinic waiting room. It surprises me that women ever date him. I can't imagine what pick-up lines Earl resorts to that would actually work on Portland girls. I envision him coming out of a bar and just turning to the nearest woman on the street and saying, *get your fine self in my Ford F-150, you perfect ten pretty.*

"Interesting fantasies you have. We'll need to talk about them at a more appropriate time. Maybe when our dead frozen colleague isn't in the room with us."

"Whenever, my stubborn friend. For the moment of truth is almost here," Earl proclaimed.

"Stubborn? I'm a lot of things right now, but stubborn isn't one of them."

"You are so darn stubborn you'd argue with a fence post. Jerry Weissman defines stubbornness. You need to learn manners and patience. If you ever have a son I suggest you spend some time in Alabama so he can learn some bona fide charm."

"Well, excuse me if I'd rather see my son be a successful businessman instead of a NASCAR driver. So what if he doesn't learn to kill his own food, and if the fur coat he gives to his mother isn't handmade? Perhaps, he won't consider barbecue pork chops as gourmet dining, and he won't think Graceland is a holy shrine. He'll have to become versed in social graces through some other approach.

Anyway, maybe I'm destined to have only daughters."

"Sure hope for your sake that doesn't happen."

"Why do you say that?"

"When you have a son you only have to worry about one penis. If you have a girl, you have to worry about everybody's penis. Here's another thing you should consider – lay off rural Southerners. You think that being cultured signifies intelligence, but you're mistaken. Sophisticated city folks don't understand why we love the communities we hail from. Generations of my family lived on the same plot of land. When you are planted in a place so long, you grow roots. Those are my people you're talking about. Respect that. "

Earl never shrank from the self-assurance that who he was, was more than good enough. I admired that aspect of him. My attempts to degrade him as a redneck only boomeranged back into my insecurities. Just when you think you know Earl, he always teaches you more about tenacity and virtue.

Looking at us through the control room's thick Plexiglas window, Savannah spoke to us via the intercom. "Sorry, this computer is slower than molasses. Should only take another minute then she'll be cooking."

Unlike CT scans or X-rays, it's safe to stay in the MRI room when it is scanning. MRI scanners don't use radiation. They are complicated machines that run enormous amounts of electricity through huge magnets to create an extraordinarily powerful magnetic field. The magnetic field is so strong that the hydrogen atoms in your body actually absorb energy. Your hydrogen atoms start to spin at a specific frequency when they absorb that energy. The dictionary definition of the physics term "resonance" is a 'particle reaction that causes excitation and internal motion in the system'. That is how Magnetic Resonance Imaging got its name. The hydrogen atoms in our cells release their excess stored energy when the hydrogen atoms are spinning. A computer collects those energy signals. The computer software then interprets those signals, and ultimately provides us with images of the body based on the magnetic energy of our hydrogen atoms.

"Here we go," said Savannah.

The vroom and clicking sound of the 15,000-pound scanner started revving. I hadn't taken my eyes off Earl for more than a moment since we left his house. His denim jacket pocket started rising up even though his hands were at his sides. It could only mean one thing. We looked at each other and screamed in unison, "Metal!!"

As I said, the MRI magnets that weigh several tons are so powerful that they change the way hydrogen spins in your body. The magnets will instantly erase credit cards in the room. You can imagine what happens when there is metal in the room. Metal objects will fly at high velocity into the open MRI tube where the body is being imaged. Metal pocket pens have been known to severely injure patients. There have even been tragic fatal cases of metal objects killing patients in the scanner. This is especially dangerous if a negligent radiology technician forgets to remove a patient's oxygen tank from the room.

I was hitting the deck as a metal gun flew rapidly towards Tarini. The chamber discharged and the bullet ended up hitting Earl. The bullet went into his right thigh sixteen inches above where I shot him in the leg.

"Fuuucck!" Earl screamed, as he rolled over in agony.

Like a monkey trying to restrain a maimed elephant, I jumped on top of Earl. Savannah turned off the MRI and ran into the room. She pulled me off Earl, screaming, "What the hell is going on here?"

Huffing and puffing I turned to Savannah and said, "I think he meant to kill me with that gun, Savannah. He probably would have killed you next."

Working through the fresh pain and squirming on the ground, Earl said, "Are you crazy?! I didn't even know I had it. Do you really think I would have brought a metal gun into an MRI room knowingly? It's Jerry's gun, Savannah. I took it off of him after he shot me in the leg." Earl pulled up his pant leg to show her the bandage from the prior wound.

"That's why you've been limping?" asked Savannah, as she looked at me.

"I did shoot him, Savannah, but he's done some bad things."

She blushed and candidly remarked, "I don't know what you boys have gotten into, but whatever it is, you shudenoughta have done it. Doctors shooting other doctors, a dead doctor on the scanner table! That is it, I'm out of here."

"No!" Earl screamed sincerely. "Now don't go getting clouded up on me, Savannah. Listen, We've bitten off more than we can chew with this one. But, we've got to get the MRI of her brain done tonight. I've got to prove there's a tumor in her brain. If we don't get it done, then the cops will start an investigation. I'm sorry to get you involved, but like it or not, you are involved. We don't know how to run the computer, and solving this situation is about having the right tool for the job. Just get us the images, and leave. That's all I'm asking."

Savannah stood there for about half a minute. Earl and I watched her every expression, just praying she would stay. Finally she wryly quipped, "Nobody's perfect. Every dog gets a few fleas now and then. But, once we get the images, I'm gone. Understand?"

TWENTY-FOUR

An MRI of the head takes about half an hour to complete.

Earl was pretty well wounded. He didn't lose much blood, but walking any distance at all with two bullet wounds was out of the question.

"I'll go find a wheelchair for you once the images are complete."

"Jerry, I just want you to know that when this is all done, it has been the worst twenty-four hours of my life. I should also let you know that everybody has the right to be an idiot, but you are starting to abuse that right."

"Just think, when the images show a malignancy, you can go home and take the rest of the week off. I'll even provide you with a doctor's note," I asserted in a flippant manner.

I knelt down beside him and did a quick evaluation of his leg. There was an exit wound in the back of his thigh. I found the bullet several moments later next to Tarini's head in the scanner. Earl was once again lucky that the bullet just missed the bone. His luck was my luck, since hitting the bone would mean surgery. Surgery for a bullet wound, by law, means there will be a criminal investigation.

Earl's discomfort was obvious from his strained facial muscles.

"Remind me to cancel my drug talk tomorrow night," he said.

Earl, like many physicians, makes portions of his income by giving lectures on the latest and greatest medications. Pharmaceutical companies often invite doctors to posh restaurants for a free gourmet meal and all-you-can-drink in order to plug their newest medication. The problem being that the latest really isn't always the greatest.

"Maybe this is a sign that you should stop being a drug whore."

"Drug whore? Drug whore? Boy, are you now calling me a prostitute?"

"It's just a figure of speech. I didn't mean to offend."

"Didn't mean to offend? Has it escaped your mind that I'm lying on cold ground with two bullet holes in my leg? Perchance I am a little sensitive right now. Your comments are about as welcome as a skunk would be at a lawn party. But… But, I do need to get my mind off the pain. So let's just get this argument over with. What is your beef with my lecturing?"

"I just feel that the pharmaceutical industry has been dishonest with America. The lectures that doctors give, as you know, are not entirely honest. They focus on the positives and don't talk enough about the negatives"

Earl slid himself towards the corner of the room, then sat up and propped his back against the wall. He let out a grunt of anguish.

"The pharmaceutical industry provides us with some of the best breakthroughs and treatments available. Don't you want to cure cancer?"

Even Earl should've known better than to use that line. That is the justification the industry uses all the time to convince citizens and politicians that their outrageously enormous profits benefit everybody.

"Ah, yes - is that what they are doing? Has any cancer drug been listed in the top fifteen selling drugs any time in the past decade? Of course not. The drugs the companies make money off of have little to do with curing cancer. In fact, the top selling drugs are the newest antacids like Nexium, or antidepressants like Paxil and Lexapro. We shouldn't forget about the erection pills. Let's face it, companies know consumers will pay more to maintain a stiffy than they will to cure cancer. And, when there is a breakthrough in cancer or AIDS, who paid for the nuts and bolts research? The drug company? No way man. The research is done at the National Institute of Health and at university labs. The funding is provided by grants from the United States government with money collected from the taxpayers. When a remarkable discovery is made, as in AIDS, and it goes on the market, how much does a year's supply cost? Many thousands of dollars that only the rich can afford. Ironically, that's only for Americans. The drugs are sold much cheaper to the Europeans and Canadians, who didn't fund the research with tax money."

Earl contested my argument, "All valid points. But, I have nothing to do with any of that. I am an oncologist and educate doctors only about cancer drugs. Besides, what's wrong with letting a guy have a little something to maintain some wood? What is so wrong with treating depression?"

"Nothing. Absolutely nothing. Except that the whole damn system is completely full of hypocrisy, as you well know. People who take antidepressants can't get erections because the drugs cause impotence. But, don't fear. The pharmaceutical industry has a remedy at the cost of $10 per an erection. Even more hypocrisy occurs with the standards set by the DEA in legalizing medication. Our very competently run Drug Enforcement Agency has no problem approving addictive substances like Xanax to help anxiety, or Oxycontin for pain. However, God forbid someone should want to smoke a joint to relieve pain. If they do that, they are viewed as lowlife drug addicts, who give money to the criminal farmers and dealers. It's much better to give money to legal entities like billion dollar corporations. They are far more honest than the dope farmer in Kentucky working his land, because pharmaceutical companies are all about finding the next cure for cancer."

Earl replied, "O.K. Again, some good points. Some loose ends, but an overall good argument. First of all we live here in Oregon. So it is legal to smoke a joint for medical reasons. Second of all..."

Savannah entered the room and interrupted him. "Well boys, glad to see you're all friends again. The images are on the computer. Just turn the power knob to off when you're all done, honey-pies. See ya."

Earl was holding his thigh and staring intently at me. "Go ahead, have a glimpse."

TWENTY-FIVE

I walked briskly into the control room and sat at the computer command station.

"Holy shit," I muttered. Our maniacal pursuit to verify the truth provided the required evidence. The digital image struck me with the intensity of a physical blow. Science had never disconnected me from sensitivity to others' suffering – my life circumstances could be blamed for that. The glioblastoma was extensive. Facts speak for themselves, and it was time to shed another layer of skin and admit my wrongs. A dreaded brain malignancy with all its misery was staring me in the face, undoubtedly akin to how Tarini's eyes had fixated on the image when she saw her films. MRI machines are lucky they don't have a conscience. The amount of devastating news they expose with definitive accuracy would be too burdensome for anything other than a machine to live with.

Seeing that MRI of a dear colleague elicited my deepest fears. A desire to be blind to the knowledge of whatever will eventually kill us is a commonly shared human trait. Most of us are able to live out our lives without the intrusion of that knowledge. But Tarini, at such a young age, had no choice in the matter. Death has an insatiable yearning for our flesh and sooner or later calls out to everyone. The Reaper called loudly for Tarini. The Reaper can capture whomever, whenever.

Non-scientists usually have a minimal understanding of the biology of cancer, but it's not a difficult concept at the basic levels. The human body is a structure that houses exceptional machines called organs such as kidneys, liver, brain, etc. Each organ performs different functions because it is constructed of tiny, unique building blocks called cells. No structure can last forever, and like the Titanic, the World Trade Center, the stars and planets, organs will eventually perish. Organs may die because of poisoning, as in the case of alcoholic liver disease. Cells can also set into motion a sequence of self-destruction called cancer. If a single cell makes a mistake in dividing to produce the next generation of cells, that mistake will continue to be passed on logarithmically to all future generations of cells within the organ. These poorly made cells can't function like the other good cells, so they just clump together and form tumors.

These cancerous tumors are bullies that push on the good cells and kill them. Then the tumors start pushing on nerves, producing terrible pain. Eventually, these cells break off from the tumors and travel through the blood stream to live in other areas of the body. If, for example, the metastasis goes to your lungs and kills off your lung tissue, you will not be able to breathe. Tarini had witnessed this process hundreds of times, and had decided that fate was not for her. It probably wasn't only about fear. Maybe it was courageous to live her life and plan her death on her own terms, although to me, she still seemed like a tree chopped down before its time, even if her leaves were wilting fast. Either way, perishing while young, with ambition, seems crueler than dying old and full of memories.

I marveled that Tarini functioned as well as she did with that monster in her brain. The human spirit will never cease to amaze. She demonstrated dignity at every moment, even when her tumor caused her to drop a fork or forced an unrestrainable wink.

Noble character and class has to be cultivated. Tarini had once explained to me that she wasn't born with the unshakable confidence she displayed. Until her late adolescence she had a bed wetting problem. Sleepover parties were her Achilles heel. After a scattering of humiliations, Tarini overcame the distressing predicament. Not by solving her lack of bladder control, but rather by spending the entire night pinching herself so she wouldn't fall asleep. No doubt it was an effortful solution, but it worked. Devising such a solution, and finding the determination to carry it through, built a refined temperament.

Earl was still in the scanner room. He screamed at me, "See! I told you you've been barking up the wrong tree. Don't worry about these here bullet wounds. We'll just look at them as memories of our friendship. Kind of like when lovers carve their initials in a tree."

I walked back into the scanner room. Father always told me, *it's important to learn how to be a winner in this world, but it's just as important that you also learn how to lose.* That lesson was something my father understood even though he could never successfully merge it with his own intellect. He knew if I could incorporate the occasional loss into my life, such acceptance would assist me immensely. There are so many roads to travel down, and suddenly I realized that despite his personal demons, he had always tried to put me on the right one. The road behind me was full of accidents, while the ones ahead were wide open. For a few moments, I took some time to think about that, and appreciated I lost Tarini to death, but could still win back friendship with Earl in life. Like so many arguments the two of us have had, the issue was not about one of us being wrong and the other right. The issue, once again, was our failure of not seeing eye to eye.

"Earl, I mean this with every molecule in my body. I'm sorry. I'm really sorry."

My apology was not a concession that killing Tarini was completely justified. Rather, my apology was an acknowledgement of putting his career in jeopardy by the haphazard shenanigans we just undertook. My apology was also an acknowledgement of incorrectly not believing him about her cancer, and for shooting him over a major misunderstanding of motivation.

"Uh, huh. O.K. then. One, give me back my damn cell phone."

"It's in the glove compartment. I put it in there after I helped you out of the car. I didn't want to bring metal into the MRI room. That could be dangerous."

"Uh, huh. Second thing, get her poor body back to the morgue before we get in more trouble. Then find me a wheelchair to get the hell out of…"

The hospital overhead paging system cut him off.

'DOCTOR WEISSMAN STAT TO ICU. DOCTOR WEISSMAN STAT TO ICU.'

I realized my digital pager wasn't with me and wondered how many important pages may have been missed. My usual sense of responsibility had been slipping. Complaining about pages can be a nonstop activity for doctors, but a segment of our psyche actually appreciates feeling needed. Realizing the overhead page was a last ditch effort to find me, I felt obligated to get to the Intensive Care Unit.

Earl hollered at me, "Jerry! I don't give a shit if someone is bleeding out of every orifice of their body up there in that ICU. You get Tarini and me out of here first."

Analogous to wild animals solely concerned with their existence, Earl was prone to showing little interest in the predicaments of others.

Nonetheless, at that moment he had a point, even if he didn't care about the shared collective benefits of graciousness to all creatures. The trouble to our personal and professional lives would be immense if we were caught. Besides, I knew who the patient crashing in the intensive care unit would be. At the time I had only one patient in the ICU, and neither the Lord nor I could save her.

TWENTY-SIX

I put Tarini back in her frozen tomb. Then I feebly pushed Earl's wheelchair to my car. Moisture evaporating from the hood produced a spooky illusion. When he was comfortably settled in the passenger seat, I told him, "Wait here."

"Be quick, and no more funny business," he answered. Like a dog recently beaten by its owner, he did not fully trust me.

By the time I arrived in the ICU the nurses were doing chest compressions on my patient. Dr. Stover had come up from the ER to run the CODE BLUE. The charge nurse informed me that there hadn't been a palpable pulse or blood pressure for twenty minutes. Only a few weeks ago, in the same exact room, I had enormous success saving a sixty-year-old prisoner we admitted from the Columbia River Correctional Institution. He had a massive heart attack, but we were able to stent open the coronary arteries in time to re-establish good blood flow to his heart muscle. After he regained consciousness, the prisoner told me he wished we hadn't saved him. He explained he was in prison for life, and didn't want to extend the misery. That seemed completely logical to me. Too bad we weren't having a similarly rewarding outcome with the CODE BLUE emergency in front of us.

The daughter was standing outside the room. She was tapping her left chest with her open right hand. Her face imparted a murky look of dismay. Reflection and rumination were accelerating towards a dark ending she unwillingly endured. Her desperation was all too familiar to those working in the intensive care unit. During a CODE BLUE, family members also become suffering patients. Dr. Stover gestured that it was o.k. for me to leave the room and address the daughter.

"Even if your mom survives this, her quality of life will be unbelievably poor. Would she want this? Honestly ask yourself, would she want this?"

"No. She wouldn't want that, but it don't matter. I can't let her go down like this. She my momma."

As the daughter and I looked at each other, I heard a nurse in the background recite the robotic sequential cardiac arrest protocols the American Heart Association had formalized in every hospital.

Two milligrams of epinephrine given.
One amp bicarb infused.
One milligram atropine infused and second milligram being drawn now.
Patient remains with no pulse, no palpable blood pressure.
The total code time now twenty-six minutes.
Normal saline remains wide open via a left antecubital 18-gauge.

"She is your mom, and we all realize she is a very special woman. Think about what you just said. Your mother trusted you to make her most important life and medical decisions for her. You said you know she wouldn't want this. Ethically you must follow the decision that your mother would want. Don't go against her wishes in her time of need."

She was still patting her chest with her right hand, and stuck out her left hand to wave me off as she gazed towards the ground at her feet. She then abruptly sat on the ground, put her hands to her face and started sobbing.

"Oh lord!! Oh, lord!" she cried. I sat down next to her and put my arm on her shoulder to comfort her. Looking at the multitude of hospital staff in the patient's room, I recognized the sense of urgency had vanished. Adrenaline flows through our veins during the first twenty minutes of a CODE BLUE, when resuscitation is possible. After twenty minutes of asystole (no pulse) in a room temperature body, there are no complete recoveries. The nurses and respiratory therapists were looking at me for direction. They needed a doctor's order for the next step.

"Call the code," I told the charge nurse who was watching us.

She announced, "Time of death is 8:06 p.m." and with that, the crowd ceased all futile efforts.

PART TWO – UNINTENDED CONSEQUENCES

TWENTY-SEVEN

I got back to my vehicle sometime later. For a moment I thought Earl was crying, then realized the wet glass just made it seem that way. Earl was on his cell phone but hung up quickly as I opened the driver's door.

"Grant wants us to come over. He's sure torn up about her, Jerry. To be honest, your accusations about killing her have not helped him to deal with this. Also, there's more things you still need to know." A moment later, Earl heard my cell phone's definitive ring and immediately said, "Hell no, Jerry. You're not talking to *her* now."

"I have to get it. It will be quick."

I've programmed a special ring on my cell phone just for my mother. After learning the British Broadcasting Company (BBC) had played the opening notes of Beethoven's Fifth at the beginning of news broadcasts during World War II to update the Allies, I decided it would serve my purposes as well. The radio station had a couple reasons for choosing the Fifth. One, it's an attention grabbing piece of music. Two, it has a hidden meaning that probably Beethoven himself was not aware of. The Morse code for V is *dot-dot-dot-dash,* which is very similar to the opening bars of the Fifth Symphony, *duh-duh-duh-dum*. To the allies, the song symbolized V for victory. When Mother calls, I also pray for victory.

Mom calls me at least once every other day. Sometimes she needs the answer to a 'major crisis' such as whether or not her friends are correct about the benefits of the Atkins diet. Or, she has found the *perfect doctor job* that I *would just love,* which always happens to be located in New Jersey, where she lives. Or maybe she's found another *perfect woman* I should meet.

My mother is always searching for the perfect woman for me. She has specific criteria. The single most important one is that the prospect be Jewish. This is even more important than whether or not the fantasy daughter-in-law is actually single. To be sure, Mother has never tried to set me up with a married woman, but she wouldn't hesitate to interfere in a relationship whose knot hasn't yet been tied.

The Other Face Of Murder

Many times she has started her descriptions of potential blind dates with, *Jerry, I am telling you she is delightful, a real sweetheart. Her mother tells me her boyfriend is a shlump. We think you'd be a much better match for her.* Of course, it's best if the woman who is fated to conceive my offspring also lives in Jersey. It is of little importance to my mother that I could already be dating somebody.

A rabbi once jokingly explained to me the difference between Catholics and Jews regarding their views on abortion. Catholics see the fetus as a human being as soon as it is conceived. Jews don't consider the fetus a human until it graduates from medical school. In truth, my mother will see me as her developing fetus until I have a wife and kids.

While it might seem logical to ignore her calls, the reality is my cell phone and pager will then ring every ten minutes until I return the call. If I ignore those modalities, she starts calling my secretary and the hospital operators. When I ask her why she needs to call every ten minutes she'll say, "I've been so worried you didn't answer! Maybe you were in trouble or dead. How should I know?" Her panic about unanswered phone calls was an aftermath of my father's death. He didn't answer his cell phone all day, and later that evening the police showed up at the house with the news.

I answered the phone. "Hello, Mom, I'm fine. But listen, I'm in the middle of something right now. I'll call you back tomorrow first thing."

"What is so important you shouldn't have time for your mother right now?"

"Nothing, Ma, I just have to go."

"Nothing? You have to get off the phone for nothing?"

All Jewish doctors agree that the most common genetic disease passed by Jewish mothers to their children is called guilt. They also say that the difference between a Pit Bull Terrier and a Jewish mother is that the Pit Bull eventually lets go.

"It's just that I'm pulling into a friend's driveway. Call me in an hour and we'll talk." With that, I hung up before the protest commenced.

TWENTY-EIGHT

Grant didn't have to ask what happened at the hospital. He immediately recognized the change in my demeanor. He handed me a letter written in Tarini's unmistakable penmanship.

"Dearest loved ones,
    Maybe you have come to find strength in my words after my death.
    Fate unfortunately intervened to take my life at an early age. Just one more reminder, that despite our desire to guide destiny, random events will ultimately pilot the course of human existence. Please be assured that I have chosen to die on my own terms. It is with trust and faith that I asked my friends to help me. I pray they will be successful in assisting me to achieve everlasting peace and comfort. My fears of death are very real. My fears of continuing life with progressive loss of my ability to think and function are even more horrifying. The future of my disease is well known to me as a physician. I have zero desire to follow a path of misery. It is my human right to have the autonomy to choose a quick and peaceful death.
    The burden I have placed on my lover, Grant, and my best friend, Earl, is unimaginable. It is only after my solicitation and diligent pleading that they have agreed to fulfill my final request. I asked only to be ignorant of the time and manner of my death, and prayed that it could be accomplished with total lack of pain and fear. Part of my last request is that the world will also be merciful towards these truly great men.
    I have enjoyed life intensely, particularly, in the last few years. There have been periods of situational depression from heartbreaking and cataclysmic life events, but it has been through love and friendship that I found meaning and hope. It is I who will miss you.

With eternal love,
Tarini

"I understand, man. You did the right thing," I told Grant, with a heavy tongue. I can't say that's exactly how I really felt. Does loving the executioner change matters? The complexities of assisting with death were becoming more challenging for me to think about. Perhaps assisting the already dying in extreme circumstances is on occasion justified. I'm just not sure Tarini's situation was an extreme circumstance. Assisting in death is a slippery slope; paradoxical, amoral and unintended consequences may be discovered at the bottom, after it's too late. This is true even when the intentions are genuinely good.

Most people are surprised to learn that Dr. Joseph-Ignace Guillotin invented the guillotine because he opposed the death penalty. Recognizing there was no way to prevent executions in 18th century France, Dr. Guillotin reasoned that the invention of a fast, painless, killing machine was at least an improvement over the even more horrific means of execution that existed in his day. His good intentions resulted in France passing a law in 1791 that everyone receiving the death penalty would be decapitated. While it was meant to be a humane form of beheading, it can be easily argued that the simplicity and speed of the guillotine increased the frequency of killing. More than fifteen thousand heads rolled by 1799.

Grant was submerged in reflection. "Her headaches were severe enough to elicit tears. They were increasing in frequency and potency."

After several moments of silence Grant again spoke up. "We know the reality of the world. Prosecutors don't gently turn away when breaking the law results in death. At first, we tried to get Tarini to explore legal physician assisted suicide under the Oregon Death with Dignity law. The confines of the law didn't work for her. Her cancer was of the brain. Under the state law, a person can only commit suicide if that person is thinking clearly at the time of the act. Tarini knew that with time the cancer was going to destroy her cognition. In addition, she didn't want to know the time, place, or method. So, we devised a strategy to make the death look natural, as if it were the result of an epileptic seizure due to her brain cancer. I figured the glioblastoma would be found, the cause of death identified, and the case would be closed. We didn't know her family wouldn't consent to a brain autopsy. I needed to do this for Tarini, and I know Earl feels the same way. How could I not fulfill the last request of the woman I love? There would be no way to live with myself."

Earl chirped in, "I could have lived with myself, but I don't feel any remorse for helping her. The whole thing did, at first, make me more nervous than a jackrabbit running up a hot steep roof. I've been involved with other confidential cases where I've assisted terminal patients to die, at their request. Those cases were much easier because we controlled the setting. Also, I must admit Tarini was at an earlier stage of her disease than anyone I've previously assisted. But the fact remains that she was a very intelligent woman who knew her devastating fate and knew what she wanted. The girl wasn't trying to hurt others, she was thinking about herself. Some call that selfish, I call it an insightful prerogative. When eternal rest is the only happiness one can hope for, the situation is desperate. Exceptional circumstances can call for extreme measures. We've all been caught up in the niggling details, but it was the overall picture for Tarini that we needed to focus on."

The one thing that still disturbed me deeply was that Tarini seemed to have a scary and uncomfortable death. Exactly what her letter begged to avoid. Suffocation while being aware of your surroundings cannot be anything short of terrifying. I delicately asked, "Do you think she was aware during her dying process?"

Grant seemed eager to ease my conscience. "That's what I really wanted to explain to you. I knew you wouldn't believe us if you didn't believe the glioblastoma existed. Like I said, you could only deal with one piece of the pie at a time."

Earl narrated the circumstances. "We really were not planning to do the whole thing at your house. Shit, it was your misfortune and ours that it went down like that. We never really had much of a plan at all. All we knew is that it had to be fast and painless. As Tarini was going to bed, she had another big seizure. Grant was pretty upset and came to ask for my help. When the seizure stopped she was in a deep postictal state."

Suddenly, I experienced a fraction of the emancipation my heart had been looking for since the night she died. A *postictal state* is a common condition of spacey unawareness that occurs after major seizures. The postictal state can last anywhere from twenty minutes to twenty hours. Epileptic patients will report that they have no memory of events that happen just after a big seizure. A seizure is an extensive electrical storm in the brain. During a seizure you, in a sense, blow your fuse box. Until you reset the fuse box there just isn't enough power to run the circuits. This creates a state of moderate anesthesia. If Tarini were in such a postictal state, she wouldn't have known what was happening to her or around her. She died pain free, and quickly, just as she asked.

Grant concluded the story. "Earl mentioned that he had a paralytic agent in his doctor's bag in his car. We quickly discussed that it might be the ideal moment. When would we be together to fulfill the mission she gave us in such an unequaled setting? It was Earl's swift thinking that we would need to conceal any trace of a needle puncture."

That there had been a lack of cold and calculated premeditation eased my mind. It was also nice to think that they didn't purposefully involve Karen and me in a contrived scheme to do it at our house. My tense muscles began to relax. The dull ache in the posterior of my head abated. Taking full deep breaths I stood up and meditatively paced the rooms in Grant's house. I went over to the refrigerator and opened the door. Then closed it. Then opened it again and grabbed a cold green apple. The apple was as sour as the week I'd had. Even so, I probably would have enjoyed it, but the overbearing da-da-da-dum ring of Beethoven's Fifth distracted me from finishing it.

TWENTY-NINE

"Hi, Mom."

"Jerry, what is going on over there? You said you'd call in an hour, but an hour goes by and there is no call."

"No, Ma. I told *you* to call me in an hour."

"Why? Don't *you* have time to call me?"

"It's not that. It has just been a difficult few days."

"Why? Are you very busy at work? Remember to eat well, no matter how busy you are. It's very important, Jerry. You need good nutrition or you'll catch a cold. You must stay away from caffeine as well. It's a drug like any other. You don't do the drugs, do you Jerry?"

"No. No. Of course not, Mom."

"So what is it? Tell your mother."

I hesitated. The less she knows, the easier my life is. On the other hand, she suspected something was going on. If I didn't tell her something, she'd continue calling until I confessed.

"A friend of mine passed away."

"Oh my gawd! Oh my gawd! Tell me, who was it?"

"It was my friend, Tarini."

"Oh my gawd! I remember her. I met her last time I visited you in Portland."

"Yes, that's right. She met us for lunch on 23rd street at Papa Haydn."

"Yes! Yes! The desserts were so decadent at Papa Haydn. I remember she wouldn't eat dessert and I thought showing such control was admirable. Wonderful girl. Wonderful girl. She wasn't for you, but a wonderful girl."

"That she was, Mom."

"How come you waited to tell me such things, darling?"

"You know, Mom; it's just hard to talk about."

"You must talk about these things. You can't keep it all inside. You're like your father, he kept everything inside. It ate him up little by little. By the end he was a nobody, a shlump."

"Ma, how can you say that about Dad?"

"What? What is it that I said? I loved the man. It's just he kept everything inside and it drove him meshugeh. If he had spent more time talking with me it would have been a blessing for him."

"Yes, I'm sure that more discussions with you would have been very therapeutic. It just wasn't his nature to talk much."

"Enough about your father. He's dead, God bless his soul. You are the one I need to worry about now. You want that I should schlep to Portland to provide support during your ordeal?"

"Oh shit," I accidentally whispered out loud in a fit of anxiety.

"What? Jerry, what's wrong?"

"Nothing, Ma, I just stubbed my toe and it hurts."

"Fine, so sometimes you're a klutz, but what's with the language? I raised you better than that."

"I'm sorry, Ma; it's just that I'm so tired. Can I call you in the morning?"

"Of course you can call me, my bubbee. Get some rest. You need your sleep or you'll get sick."

The thought of her visiting Portland during such an overextended period of my life resulted in a shoddy night of sleep.

Da-da-da-dum. Da-da-da-dum.

The bedside alarm clock read 6:02 a.m.

"Hello," I answered in a scratchy voice that hadn't warmed up to the day.

"I wanted I should catch you before work," said Mother.

Years ago, I learned that it's entirely possible to love somebody without always liking them. As I lifted my head up from the pillow, I noticed a dark circular stain of drool. "My first patient isn't until ten, Mom."

"I've been up for hours. I've been so worried about you, and thinking about your poor friend, Tarini. How hard it especially must be for her poor mother. My GERD was acting up all night. What should I take?"

"Take a Tums."

It doesn't bother me that family and friends always ask for medical advice, but the over-medicalization of our society has been a disappointing trend in modern medicine. I would bet that if ten random fifty-year-olds were examined by me, I could find an underlying disease process in at least eight of them. Being given a clean bill of health by a doctor, means the doctor did not perform an adequate work-up. In recent decades we've lowered the guidelines for what should be considered high blood pressure, which has resulted in numerous more patients with the diagnosis of hypertension. The amount of glucose allowed in the blood has been lowered, so millions more can be referred to as diabetics needing expensive drugs. Even mild amounts of cholesterol in the blood are considered by many to be a serious disease. Everything is a disease. Simple heartburn is now called Gastric Esophageal Reflux Disease or GERD. Once diagnosed with GERD, people like my mother are convinced they have a serious disease process. People can even choose to see a GERD specialist to help them live with their disease. After an expensive work-up, the patient goes on a three-dollar a day drug to prevent heartburn. What do the billions of people around the world do without GERD specialists and expensive medication? - They live with some heartburn! Not only that, they will also make the necessary changes such as eliminating certain foods that exacerbate the problem, or not eating just before bed. Whatever it takes. Not Americans; we'll just take the pill.

"A Tums? I took my Prilosec already. A simple Tums will help?"

"I don't know, Ma."

"You're a doctor, and you don't know?"

"We don't know everything."

"I should say. Apparently not."

A slight panic ensued as I looked at the bedside clock. Klaus will be calling the cops in less than three hours. How did I forget about Klaus? He had to be tracked down immediately.

"Gotta go, Mother."

"What? You have to go? You just said you don't have to be at work until ten. You don't sound well, Jerry."

There's only one way to get off the phone fast with Mom. "I'll call you in a few hours."

THIRTY

"It iz murder," Klaus said, after I gave him the true story. The stress of the past days had put limitations on my patience.

"Murder? A few decades ago your country developed eugenics! Your country killed off anybody with a mental disability ranging from retardation to depression. The only reason France has so many tree-lined streets is because Germans liked to march in the shade after murdering its citizens. Your country destroyed its European neighbors without a second thought. Germany killed any undesirable minority including my grandparents. You know damn well what murder is, Klaus, and this isn't murder."

I can't say that argument sweetened him up. Ripping on his homeland probably wasn't the best way to plead the case.

"I hail from ze greatest nation! Vee invented gaz-powered motorzyclez, ze X-ray, and Mizter Levi Strauzz gave uz ze blue jeanz. Do not uze our inventionz if you hate Germanz zo much."

There was only one way to get Klaus to not call the police, and it wouldn't be by pointing out that Levi Strauss was a Jew. I would have to make him feel like the winner, and couldn't let my pride get in the way. The stakes were too high. I would have to resort to lies and manipulation. Mother once told me it would be important to have a viable alternative if medicine or law didn't work out. That fallback was to be another famous Jewish actor, like Dustin Hoffman or Kirk Douglass. Finally, those after-school drama classes my mother encouraged me to take were about to pay off.

Solemnly I pleaded, "You're absolutely one hundred percent correct, Klaus. In fact, when I cut on the Germans, I'm only cutting on myself. Part of my family on my mother's side was German. It was only through the extraordinary courage and generosity of the German citizens who hid them that any of them survived. Letting one madman's moment in history take away from an entire country is simply not fair. If the whole world had the strong work ethic of the German people, there would be fewer problems. In fact, I attribute all my personal success to the genes I've inherited from my mother's side of the family. We also must remember that if Wilhelm von Roentgen (a name we all learn in medical school) had not invented the x-ray, we would have never even solved this case. The MRI is a machine that could only have been contrived after the greatest of all medical technologies was first invented. We must think about how many lives have been saved as a result of German medical innovations."

Klaus rubbed his chin slowly; then answered, "Zat iz correct."

"So my thinking about Tarini is this. No major harm was done. She was going to die anyway. The intention was only to end suffering. If we get authorities involved, no good can come from it. We will all have many questions to answer, such as why we didn't tell them about the Vecuronium immediately. We can try lying, but will our colleagues in the chemistry lab also lie? It would be so much easier to let life go on without the hassles. There is a German saying 'to bury the hatchet,' isn't there?"

"Yez my friend. Daz Kriegzbeil begraben."

I repeated, "Das Kriegsbeil begraben."

"Yez! Daz Kriegzbeil begraben!"

And that was the end of that.

THIRTY-ONE

I went back to Grant's house to keep him company. Religion has never been a central focus in my life, but religious tradition remained important to me in times of need. One of those traditions is 'sitting shiva'. While mourning is universal, the actual methods of mourning vary considerably between cultures. Derived from the Hebrew word for 'seven', shiva is a Jewish ritual in which the family honors the deceased for seven days. Friends are expected to visit and comfort the mourners during that period. My plan was to stop by Grant's house every day for at least seven days. Grant wasn't Jewish, and therefore he wouldn't consciously experience the week as a mourning ceremony, but it was important to me. I felt it would be up to his friends to provide a process for grieving, remembering, and healing.

Sitting shiva is one of the most firmly rooted traditions in my culture. The first mention of the practice is in the Book of Genesis, when Joseph mourned his father, Jacob, for seven days. References to the tradition appear throughout the Bible. God Himself mourned for seven days after destroying the world with a flood during the time of Noah. Traditionally, Jews eat hard-boiled eggs and lentils during the first shiva meal. The round shapes signify the cyclical nature of life. I don't like eggs, and cooking lentils was too much of a chore, so I bought Grant some organic cantaloupe and honeydew melons.

While I cut up the melons in Grant's kitchen, Grant sat in the living room, staring out the window. I could faintly hear the sound of his teeth grinding. I'd have to confront him about that soon, or he would face enormous dental problems and bills, but the timing seemed inappropriate -- like telling a smoker to quit at the most tense moment in his life. I handed him a plate of melon; eating would at least temporarily cease the grinding. He never took a bite. The mellowest section of Mozart's *Jupiter Symphony No. 41,* the andante, was playing on his stereo. It intensified an already melancholy mood. I wondered if Grant's spirits would have been any better had I arrived just a few minutes earlier during the allegro section. Music's effect on the mind can be more powerful than alcohol or drugs. I was tempted to change the CD to the Beatles or something more uplifting, but on second thought, realized that such attempts to short-circuit grief are not only improper; they are doomed to fall short of the intention. There are no simplistic solutions for complex problems. Ongoing support is the proper answer for those grieving.

He told me, "There is only one thing I wish more than anything in the world. I wish it had been me instead of Tarini. If I could push a button to make that happen, I'd push it a thousand times in a minute."

"I know how you feel." And just like that, I had done exactly what I just told myself not to do. A simplistic answer for such a complex problem was ridiculously stupid.

Grant rolled his eyes at me. "Do you? Do you know what it's like to have the pain of thirty broken bones in an auto accident? I don't, and since it has never happened to me, I don't pretend to know. Unless you've felt the pain, you don't know. You simply don't know."

If he only knew a tenth of the pain I carried since the death of my father, but it wouldn't have helped to share my own problems. "Grant, that was the wrong thing to say. What can I do? Tell me, please, what can I do?"

"Believe me, there isn't a single thing. I'm helpless and hopeless," he said solemnly.

"It's okay to grieve. Just remember there are going to be better days than today. And, one good day, that's everything man. Once you have that single good day, the next good day will be around the corner. One day at a time. One hour, one minute, one second at a time. There may not be anything I can do now. In the future there will be. That's because I'm your friend."

He didn't respond. Sometimes the things people don't say have a bigger impact than what they do say. The oppressive silence gripped me, coercing my mouth to keep talking.

"Maybe I haven't been a great friend the last few days, but I've learned a lot. You mean so much to me. It's sad, but losing a friend has reinforced how much my other friends mean to me. Healing may take a while, but we will have good times again. If that doesn't happen for a couple of years, then I'll just have to wait. But, I will wait. Better must come."

Grant granted me his agreement. "Indeed, better will come."

Our eyes looked like those of allergy patients visiting a cat farm. Nothing more was said that night. The next day would be Tarini's funeral. We were both exhausted, but I don't think either of us got any sleep that night. I don't think Grant actually slept much at all since her death. To rest is defined as getting peace of mind. It would be several more days before he got rest.

THIRTY-TWO

Karen and I arrived at the funeral half an hour early. We slowly approached the grieving family. I shared stories of how their loved one had solved medical cases that several extraordinary doctors had missed. I wanted them to know how greatly their child was appreciated, but they could barely process language.

As Karen put it, the event was a Monday morning mourning. The red mahogany casket with impressive side engravings contrasted against the black suited mourners. Doctors throughout the community sent large bouquets of flowers. Only about a dozen doctors actually came to the funeral. Maybe the others couldn't leave their patients, but some people utterly dread going to funerals. They remind us that every day we are closer to the end of our lives than we have ever been in the past. We take joy in celebrating together the other milestones we reach in life. Birthdays, weddings, and Fourth of July cookouts are always well attended. When the ritual gathering is for headstones, we try to look the other way.

Earl and I didn't share many words. Just prior to the service he had whispered to me, "This whole thing is starting to give me the heebie-jeebies." I bit down on my lower lip and gave him a glance of understanding.

Then the priest started the service.

Lord our God, you are the source of life. In you we live and move and have our being.

Keep us in life and death in your love, and, by your grace, lead us to your kingdom,

Through your son Jesus Christ, our Lord.

Goose bumps rose from my flesh. A cool wind was blowing, but it was the ambience, not the weather that extracted them.

Amen.

In the name of God, the merciful Father,

We commit the body of Grant Simmons to the peace of the grave.

Two heartbreaking funerals of two dear friends in a two-week period. Grant and Tarini were in the middle of their lives. They had so much still to do, extraordinary talents that could have helped others. Looking over at Tarini's grave, at the plot next to Grant's, generated so much anguish that I felt it necessary to consciously shut out the priest when he started the *have mercy on us* routine.

Why, in hard times, is God so often portrayed as loving and merciful? On the other hand, in good times, God is portrayed as a punisher. Hellfire awaits those with sin and those without salvation. Aren't these hypocritical ways for organized religions to keep us faithful? If you're downcast, they will give you mercy. If you're happy, they will try to bring you down. How can people ever feel good about themselves? Why pride should be considered one of the seven deadly sins had always baffled me, but I see now that if you have belief in your own abilities, then you don't need God's help. If everyone had pride, it would be a disaster for organized religion. It's not the fault of God that religion has perverted His power and beauty. The war for our souls remains a war for gold.

For that matter, we humans also overrate our own strengths and authority. Grant liked the power of being a doctor, just like he enjoyed defeating an opponent in a game of chess. But, the harder they come, the harder they fall. When given the power of God to take away life, Grant used it, but became mortally humbled. In how many Greek tragedies do the Gods destroy mortals by giving them too much power? How many dictators have we seen go insane with the absolute corruption of power? Yet, so many aspire to attain power. When we do get it, it's often too hard to handle. Tarini, unknowingly cursed Grant by giving him absolute power over the fate of her own life. Unfortunately, when given authority, we are not simultaneously given wisdom.

Grant once watched his cousin Aaron suffer in severe pain from cancer for weeks, only to die anyway. The thought of watching Tarini go through a fraction of that pain must have frightened the piss out him. However, relieving her of the impending pain was not a simple act without an aftermath. The law of unintended consequences started revving up almost immediately, for all of us.

The morning of Tarini's funeral, Grant had confided to me that he also worried her death was premature. Perhaps, he felt, she could have had a good quality of life for a few months longer. I reminded him that according to her suicide note she was more than ready for dying. At the time, I didn't think excessively about his revelation to me. It turned out, divulging that concern was essentially a deathbed confessional for Grant.

Whenever people die, loved ones always ask themselves what they could have done differently. For Grant, the questions and alternative answers became unbearable. Pieces of Grant genuinely died when his lover died. Tarini was his oxygen that he himself had shut off. Their lives were entwined, and their deaths were not a loose affiliation.

Karen put it best: *Some say that God never gives people more than they can handle. The truth is He does. Tarini's plea for help was more than Grant could handle. Perhaps more than any human can handle.* Love and hope are the things that can get us through the hardest days. Grant had lost both.

His parents were faring no better. The funeral crowd listened to their heaving drifting in and out of synchrony with each other. Neither wiped the tears that dripped onto the dark garments they must have reluctantly put on that morning. Drained, Grant's mother didn't even have the fortitude to walk after the ceremony. I was one of the men who helped carry her to the waiting limo parked next to the Hearse that transported her son to the burial. I couldn't bring myself to make eye contact with her. Some sort of shame or fear, not easily explained with logic or words, possessed me.

Grant's suicide stirred-up memories of my father that can never be entirely expunged, despite my many attempts to do so. The dichotomy of both empathy and rage still lingered within me. During Grant's funeral, I came to understand that solving the mystery of Tarini's death was only a minor achievement. In a way, it was a diversion from the fire that her death reignited. The real mystery, the one that I still needed to confront, the one that continued to defy an answer, still eluded me.

My father had told us he was taking a day trip to New York City to catch up with an old friend, and take care of some unfinished business. The old man had never lied to us, and he didn't lie to us then. The friend he went to visit was the Statue of Liberty. While the statue weighs two-hundred and twenty-five tons, her actual symbolic weight in the heart of a man like my father was immeasurable. Lady Liberty was the woman he loved above all others. Even though she couldn't change his past, she provided the freedom that allowed him to choose his future. My father would have related to Tarini's letter when she wrote, "*…it is my human right to have the autonomy to choose a quick and peaceful death.*" On the ferry ride back to the mainland, he jumped overboard, and his remains were never found.

The liberty and autonomy the United States conferred upon him was something he never took for granted. After arriving here from post World War II Europe, Father never left this country once. He missed out on business deals that required foreign travel, but his conviction to never leave America was stronger than concrete. In this place, he lived free, and without the fear that impregnated his first decade of existence.

The fact that he survived the Holocaust was a daily blessing as well as a burden he carried everywhere. Although he could hardly bear to speak about it, my father's eyes often teared up at the thought of his parents' unspeakable suffering in the ghetto and concentration camp, and the misery they must have felt not knowing the fate of their only, beloved child.

This he knew. My grandparents' last thought was of him. They accepted an opportunity to have him smuggled out of the ghetto with whatever bare essentials could be fit into a backpack, knowing they would probably never see each other again. In their scramble to save my father, they never thought to pack any pictures of themselves. As an adult, he studied photos taken at the liberation of the camps, searching for their faces. The more he learned about the camps, the more vivid and recurrent were his nightmares. In the end, the nightmares manipulated and altered his few recollections of them. The hardship of their final days was all he could recall of them. Distorted memories perpetually updated with excruciating clarity.

In a way, my ability to prosper on my own was what ultimately gave my father the freedom to take his life. He had waited until I was out of medical school and could live independently. Indeed, the day he jumped into the water was the day I left all remnants of my youth behind. During his worst bouts of depression, he did everything in his power to keep going because he didn't want his son to suffer his fate of not having had parents to provide. I had always counted on him to be there for me. That was his finest quality - being there for me - and no matter how I rationalize it, it hurts now that he isn't. To this day, I cling to every piece of advice he gave me. I wish there was more, but it's what I have left.

What I do understand about my father is that, on the day I was born, he felt like he personally had won World War II. The birth of a boy meant our family survived in spite of the Nazis; they hadn't annihilated our family's name or genes. Victory would never be theirs, and that joy in his heart pulled him out of the clutches of demons that constantly tried to pull him down.

Bipolar disorder is a disease of alternating depression with manic pleasure. For many, it may be a result of chemical imbalance. That wasn't the case for my father, and it was the reason why medications were never effective for him. For my father, there were two opposing forces that pulled at him: The despondency over the pure evil of the holocaust and the ecstasy of having his own son.

The reason he stayed with my mother was also because of me. He married the wrong woman and they both eventually recognized it. When you don't have love, you'll cling to the first person who appears to love you. As time passed, my father's priority was no longer my mother. His priority was me. My mother always loved me and protected me, and that was a good enough reason for him to stay with her, because by doing so, he was staying with me.

Part of me always struggled to make him proud, even though he never put pressure on me to succeed. I wanted to show him how well I could prosper on my own. But once I achieved that goal, he decided I could live without him. Success can breed alienation. If he had seen how much I still needed him, he would have never taken his own life.

Blocking the memory of my father was essential or it would slowly erode me, just like the memory of his parents eventually destroyed him. We shared a saga of heartache, lingering ghosts that wouldn't fade away. There had to be an end for the path of self-destruction. Our family curse started with Hitler, but must end in my generation. When my children are born, they will never know about my father's suicide.

THIRTY-THREE

For a while, there wasn't an hour in the day when I wouldn't think of Grant and Tarini. That was then. Subsequently, I would purposefully reminisce on why they were important to me. A deliberate effort to focus on remembering not to forget. Life goes on, and with it new pleasures and tragedies occupy the days. However, despite the remedy of time, everyone soon realized that many uncontrollable occurrences were set in motion by the deaths of our friends.

* * *

As I brushed my teeth the morning after Grant's funeral, it was odd to feel so empty and so full at the same time. So empty because of the residual void due to Grant's absence. He was my first friend in Portland. Together, we had explored and learned from the city, which suddenly seemed a desolate place. I was also full of sadness and frustration. So full that I started to worry the pressure build-up was becoming too much, like a volcano ready to erupt. Yet, I knew then, more than ever, if I didn't quickly find some joy in life, I'd fail everybody including Grant, Tarini, Karen and myself.

"I thought Roy was acting a bit strange at the funeral yesterday," asserted Karen as she brushed her wet hair at the adjacent sink.

I spat the baking soda toothpaste into my sink, and asked, "How so?"

"Just more distant, like his mind was preoccupied with some challenge."

"I'm not sure that's unusual for Roy. He probably was thinking about how to build some invincible Dungeons & Dragons character or something. Anyway, I'm still too fixated on Grant to think about Roy."

Karen acknowledged my sentiments, but kept pushing me. "Unfortunately, the world is full of tragic individuals like Grant," she said. "One person's suicide can affect other people in the same way that slow moving water can erode even the hardest of stones over time. But Roy is more like delicate soil than hard stone. I worry it will only be a matter of time before there's another tragedy."

I continued to get dressed as Karen's words digested in my mind. After putting my wallet in my corduroy pants pocket, I sat on the couch and reached down to tie my shoes.

"I'm going with you to the airport," Karen announced as she applied some lipstick and blush. She had the type of beauty that didn't require any makeup, in my opinion.

"Maybe it would be best if you meet us for dinner. Mom is always a little frazzled after getting off a plane. Besides, I don't want you to spend more time than is essential with her."

"Jerry, everybody thinks their parents are un-cool. I'm sure I'll love her. Don't be so nervous."

"You didn't grow up around any Jewish people did you?"

"No. Why?"

"Jews are different. Everything is a big deal to a Jew. You know how you say I'm the only person you know who doesn't like to watch Seinfeld?"

"Yeah, so what about it?"

"Well, it's like watching a re-run of my childhood on TV. In every episode Seinfeld takes an extremely minor problem like a bad haircut or not getting enough exercise and goes off on the topic for the entire thirty minutes."

"It's hilarious! What's wrong with that?" Karen rarely backs down from an argument. She's right about a lot of things, but not always. The night after Grant's funeral, for instance, we picked up Chinese food for takeout. Karen left a 15% tip. There is no reason to leave a tip on takeout food. Reasoning with her that we don't leave tips at a drive-through, nor do we tip the grocery store checkout lady, was unsuccessful. Reasoning with her about her favorite television show was about as counterproductive.

"Well, nothing is wrong with it. It's just what being Jewish is all about. The writers of the show are Seinfeld and Larry David. Jewish guys who made millions by showing what life was like for them. It's also how life was for me growing up."

"So give me an example."

I wanted to use the example of my obsessive annoyance about her leaving the tip, but didn't dare go there.

"Fine. Let's take the time Mother made a side dish of sweet-potatoes. I never liked sweet-potatoes. You'd think that would be the end of it, right? But, instead there would be a full hour analysis of why I didn't want to eat her sweet-potatoes. She would start with how other kids would be so happy to have sweet-potatoes. Then the discussion would venture into how everyone in the extended family loves sweet-potatoes except Cousin Marvin. Cousin Marvin developed stomach cancer, and I should eat the sweet potatoes so I don't end up with the same fate. Now, all that wouldn't be so bad. But, it doesn't stop there. For the rest of my life, my mother will send me articles about the excellent nutrition sweet-potatoes provide. Did you know their color is a result of the high beta-carotene content? If not, my mother just sent me an article I'd be happy to let you read."

"I think that is so sweet, that she is constantly thinking about your well-being."

"Karen, seriously, every meal had some issue like that. You put three Jews at a table, and you'll have five opinions on the food. Sometimes I wish I was Tibetan. The silence of meditating all the time must be wonderful."

Karen gazed at me. "There is nothing worse than good people with good opinions keeping silent. It didn't work out for the Tibetans, and it sure as hell won't work for the Jews to keep silent. I think I'm really going to like your mother. I'll be ready to go in five minutes."

There she was, waiting for us in Baggage Claim - the woman who gave birth to me, and would never let me forget it. Not a wrinkle on her face, thanks to her plastic surgeon whom she claimed was *a miracle worker like Moses*. But I was concentrating on her hands. Veined and splotched with brownish sun spots. Hands are more dependable for revealing the age of modern American women. Each of hers grasped big brown paper bags bulging with bagels.

"Bubelah, oh my darling bubelah! How are you doing after going through so much? Tell me, how was the funeral?"

I kissed her on the cheek, and relieved her of the bagels. "You know, we also have bagels in Portland, Mother!"

Ignoring me, she turned to Karen, "Oh, is she pretty, Jerry! I'm telling you, you two could make the most beautiful baby." Not a reaction I was expecting from her about my gentile girlfriend. Maybe making a baby had transcended the being Jewish card.

Karen giggled, and stretched out her arm to shake hands with my mother. "I'm Karen, Mrs. Weissman. Jerry told me so many good things about you."

"And he should. We mothers don't get enough credit for what we provide the world. I gave the world a doctor."

"Mom, there must be over fifty bagels in these bags."

"There were seventy bagels in there before I got on the plane. I gave the man next to me one so he shouldn't go hungry. I also had half of one. I'm still hungry, but I wanted there should be enough for you."

"Mother, you could have eaten the other half. We'd be O.K. with sixty-eight bagels."

Karen was really enjoying the absurdity. I could see in her face that she was hoping the carousel workers would be slow in getting my mom's bags off the plane.

Karen pursued every angle. "Tell me Mrs. Weissman, where did you buy these bagels?"

"Oh my little sweet precious thing," as if they were already best of friends, "these come from the deli of my dear friend, Chayim. Believe me when I tell you, people travel across New Jersey to purchase his bagels and challah, the most delicious the world has ever known. His potato salad on the other hand, is a little too salty."

Whenever I visit Mother, she takes me to Chayim's Delicatessen, where the blintzes, corned beef, and cheesecake are so worth waiting for that the lines sometimes are out the door. Despite his success, I have never felt sorrier for a creature than I have for Chayim. His deli showcases loud osteoporotic women with severely sun-damaged faces. As they order the food in deep Jersey accents they invariably augment their requests with vast amounts of useless information about their lives. On my last visit, the lady ahead of me literally took fifteen minutes to place her order. She would start with the long greeting: *"Chayim, hello. How's your week? It's getting cold out, no? Let me find my list."* And while she searched for her list buried somewhere in her over-sized, disorganized purse, she gave her opinion on all the news and gossip she had read in the local paper that morning. When she finally found the list, nothing was straightforward. Every item was a commentary. *"I'll take three-pounds of salami for Joey. He* should watch his cholesterol, but he loves your salami, Chayim. You think it maybe best to do his cholesterol a favor and only take one pound? Maybe corned beef has less cholesterol than salami? What do you think? A dill pickle for Rose please. It's amazing she can still eat such pickles anymore with the condition of her teeth. Maybe I should make it two pickles since her friend may come for lunch tomorrow, what do you think, Chayim?" Of course, this woman came to do her weekly shopping at the heart of lunch hour. As the groaning line grew behind her, I could see the blood pressure visibly rise in the vessels of Chayim's forehead. "*How's the pumpernickel today, Chayim? You think I should get the small or large loaf? Little Hannah loves your pumpernickel bread. But, she didn't eat much of the bread last week. Today she asked for bread, but by today it was stale… Maybe you could slice only half the loaf? That way half of it will stay fresher longer.*"

Well, Karen's question immediately won over my mother, who was delighted to explain how so many bagels came to accompany her on the plane.

"I had intentions of buying only a dozen bagels. Then I told Chayim the story of what happened recently to your friends. At first he wasn't so interested. Eventually, I think it really touched him, because he ended up giving me two free bagels. So, I said to him how nice it was to give me fourteen bagels for the price of twelve. He told me that it was his special to me today since I'm coming to visit you in your time of need. So who am I to turn down such a special? I told him I'd take five dozen at that special price. I ended up getting seventy bagels for the price of sixty. A real bargain. You should eat them in good health."

By the time Mother was done with the bagel anecdote, her two suitcases had appeared on the carousel.

"All right then," I said, "I guess we're ready?"

Mother replied, "And what? Leave the rest of my bags?"

"How many suitcases do you have, Mom?"

"I have four."

"Four suitcases for a five day trip? I didn't think they let passengers bring that many bags on the plane."

"Apparently they don't. The lady at the counter wanted to charge me for bringing so many bags. She said it would cost $40 for every suitcase above the usual two you are allowed. Have you ever heard such nonsense? It took me a half-hour to explain to her supervisor that such behavior was highway robbery. Eventually, they told me I could take all the bags on for free. I tell you, if you don't watch out people will try to take advantage of you all the time."

Instead of arguing, I maintained self-control, and reminded myself that her arteries and mine carry the blood that ties us together, no matter how different our personalities may be. Sometimes it's best to act like a politician always trying to please, even if it's not true to your own heart.

THIRTY-FOUR

Back at the house we spent five minutes rearranging the freezer to fit our new stock of bagels. We made it through the first twenty seconds of an R.E.M. song before our new guest solicited a request.

"Jerry, turn down the music! Such loud noise irritates my pancreas."

Karen took advantage of the silence and hit the new message button on the answering machine.

Roy's rambling message came across barely audible and creepy. "I…uh…sorry. My fault. So… sorry. Brain cancer so bad, bad, very bad, my bad…"

Karen glanced at me, clearly worried that something terrible was amiss with Roy. There was no need for her to say anything; we were on the same wave length. We needed to do everything in our power to curb any thoughts of culpability Roy was having. Why he felt sorry, and how he was involved with her death eluded me at that point. Nevertheless, the fear that Roy would do something drastic, like Grant, overwhelmed us. Trying not to overreact, Karen concentrated on the glass of orange juice she was bringing to my mother.

"Jerry, do you know that man?" Mother asked.

I swallowed hard and felt a dry lump in my throat.

"Just a friend, Mother."

The next message was from Earl. "Jerry, give me a call. You ain't gonna believe the fucked up message crazy boy Roy left on my machine today."

Mother seemed shocked, "The language. What's with the language? Tell me this, what kind of person curses in such a way? Do you also call this person a friend?"

Before she even finished the question, I had dialed Earl's number. At that point it was hard to tell what hurt the most. Thinking Roy was in some way involved stung, but knowing that Earl and Grant had not been totally honest with me was just as bad. I didn't want to pry, but it did seem that I was owed a full explanation.

"Earl, what did he say?"

"Oh, you are not going to believe this one. Dumb-ass left me a message saying he is sorry for killing Grant and Tarini. The boy is crazy with a capital C. He needs more than a talking to. Next time I see him I'm going to slap him so hard his clothes will be outta style."

"Earl?"

"Yes?"

"Did Roy ever know anything about the plans to end Tarini's life? Did he have any role whatsoever?"

"Are you kidding? Hell no!"

"Did Roy know about Tarini's cancer?"

"No. Jerry, I'm telling you, the only people who knew were me and Grant. For whatever reason, she didn't even tell her parents about the cancer."

"Is that right?"

"Yes."

"Interesting that he mentioned her cancer on my answering machine. Was I the only one left out of the loop?"

"God damn it, I swear that she never told anybody other than me and Grant. At least that's what she always told us. Honestly, I have no idea how Roy could have known anything about anything."

"Did he have anything to do with Grant's death?"

"Well, I wasn't there, and obviously I didn't know Grant was suicidal. Think about it, though. Roy couldn't kill anything even if his hippy ass wanted to. The boy is so skinny he has to run around in the shower just to get wet."

"O.K. Where is he now?"

"Hell if I know. I called him and even went over to his place. The boy is missing."

"Listen, my mother is in town and…"

"Your mother? That fine looking gem you have a picture of on your piano? Well, let's go out to supper and celebrate her visit!"

"Earl, that picture was taken two decades ago. Anyway, forget about dinner, we have to find Roy."

"Ten-four buddy, what's the plan? I'll tell you that my plan was to be layin' up in the house all day to get some rest. It's been hectic enough the past few weeks and I've got a full schedule at the office tomorrow. Lately it feels as if we've been working like beavers without any pay. Seriously, we've been busier than a pair of jumper cables at one of my family reunions."

"I hear you. I actually don't have a plan anyway. Let me give an acquaintance a call to see if he can help us out."

"Let me know if I can be of assistance. Otherwise I'm pulling down the shades to make it darker than the inside of a cow, and try to get some sleep."

"How's the leg, Earl?"

"Hurts like the devil."

"Maybe we should get a surgeon to look at it," I suggested.

"Screw that. I've only had one surgery in my entire life and that was for the most important of reasons."

"What reason is that?"

"I needed a redo of my circumcision. It looked to me like the pediatrician who originally performed it, did it with his teeth."

"I can understand why you would want that fixed."

"Well to be honest, it didn't bother me that much. I was in love with this girl in my early twenties, and it really freaked her out. So I did it for her."

"Love? I never knew you'd ever been in love." Heartfelt attachment towards a woman has never been something he's talked about. Earl believes women are like a fire. Getting too close can result in a serious burn. From a safe distance, they provide warmth and comfort.

"Well, let's put it this way," he said. "At the time, I'd rather have spent four out of five nights with her than drinking beer with my buddies. So I figure that must have been love. Just because you haven't seen me in love doesn't mean it doesn't happen. Falling in love again is still something I have penciled in on my things-to-do list."

"Fascinating. You'll have to tell me more about her sometime. I'll call you when I know more about Roy."

I pulled out the card from my wallet and dialed the number.

The hoarse Italian accent was unmistakable. "Frankie Russo here, what do you need?"

"Yes, hello Mr. Russo. This is Dr. Jerry Weissman. I took care of your brother, the English Professor, several weeks back in the hospital."

"Yo, Doc, of course you did. Thank you so much for your help, son."

"How is your brother doing?"

"Well, you know he's still got the AIDS. Overall he is doing okay. He's thinking clearly and is starting to come to terms with his irrational behavior. My brother is no longer the classy guy he used to be, but what do you expect? He's back in Tennessee and writing a book about his experiences. Who knows if he'll finish it before he dies."

"That's great. It's good to hear he is doing something positive with his energy."

As Frankie talked, classic Sinatra songs played from his stereo in the background. "Positive? I suppose. Sometimes it bugs me to think of these things as positive. Only in the arts and in literature are drug addicts hailed as heroes, but real life paints a different picture. It will be a shame if some kid reads his book and gets romantic visions of doing cocaine enemas in Mexico. You follow?"

"Yep, I do. Listen, Mr. Russo, I need a favor."

"Call me Frankie. Anything you need, you name it."

"I have this friend who is missing. He's mentally unstable at the moment. Do you think you could help me in tracking him down?"

"If he hasn't fled Portland already, consider it done, Doc. Is this guy dangerous?"

"Physically speaking he is definitely no Schwarzenegger. He doesn't own a gun. He does collect samurai swords, but wouldn't know how to use one with any skill."

"What's his name?"

"Roy. Roy Quill. Some of his friends who play Dungeons & Dragons and trade comic books with him, call him Septimus Mikato-Valkus."

"Say what? You kidding me?"

"Yeah, Frankie, don't worry about it. Just go with Roy Quill."

"O.K. Roy Quill. Got it. Let me give my boys at the precinct a call and see what I can learn."

"So, Frankie, I noticed your cell phone number has a 702 area code before it."

"What of it? I live in Las Fucking Vegas. Came here after retirement. Thought I'd like the weather after so many years in the rain. You know what I'm saying? But, it's too damn hot. I don't know why they even sell thermometers that go below eighty degrees out here. Sometimes I drink hot coffee just to cool off. Swear to God, your tongue will get sunburned if you speak too much out here. I want to sell the place and move back to Portland. You have to love that town because it's more than a city. Only someone who's lived there can relate that Portland is a feeling, an entity with a soul. Maybe you can be my doc when I move back."

"Free service anytime, Frankie. A favor for a favor."

"That's what I like to hear, Doc. Who needs money anymore? It's all about fair bartering."

"I'm with you, Frank. I've always been a fan of free-trade."

"As long as you only trade with someone who knows his trade."

"Well, you know, the Talmud says, *the parent who does not teach his child a useful trade is teaching him or her to steal.*"

"Who's Thal Mood?" Frank asked.

"Nobody. It's a book called the Talmud."

"Never read it. Who wrote it?"

"A bunch of old guys. You wouldn't like it, Frankie."

"Why not? I'm an old guy. We old guys have to live with the fact that our experience and wits are the best things we've got, considering that our bodies are falling apart. Believe me, I'd rather be out chasing women than reading. At this point in my life, it's hopeless. These days *getting lucky* means I found the remote control in less than an hour. Try not to get old son, it's terrible. At this point, the clerk at the video shop won't even rent me a porno because he's worried about my heart."

As a doctor, I learned a long time ago that there is no such thing as 'the golden years'. It's a fable created by the young to make the old feel better. The average male lives until seventy-five, making our 'middle age' start at thirty-seven, not in our fifties, as depicted by the media. Aging has two stages. For the young, it's a developmental activity. In our thirties it converts to a process of gradual unraveling. Midlife begins when rock music sounds too loud, then progresses to where nobody talks loud enough.

"Well then, don't rent the really steamy videos. Go for something a little tamer."

"You got a suggestion, son?"

"How about *'Debbie Does Depends'*? I heard it's a classic." Joking about erotica seemed a bit out of place with a guy that kept calling me 'son', but Frankie's belting laugh was worth the awkwardness.

"Ho! Very funny. A doctor and comedian bundled into one brain. Listen, I'm about to burn a manicotti in the oven. Let me look into this Roy Quill character, and we'll talk later."

THIRTY-FIVE

It only took Frankie Russo about ten minutes to call me back.

"Listen; there is a report of a cruiser dispatched to the address of Roy Quill today for some sort of disturbance around 8 a.m. They never booked your friend, which can be a good thing or a bad thing."

"What would be a bad thing?"

"Perhaps they took him somewhere to rough him up. They wouldn't do that unless he was being a real asshole. I know the guys who were dispatched to the apartment. These are respectful cops."

"Well he's not an asshole. So what would be a good thing?"

"They may have just taken him to the hospital or something without arresting him."

"Can you find out for me?"

"You bet, son, but at the moment the guys that went to his address are out on a Code Seven?"

"Code Seven?"

"Yeah, it means they're at lunch."

"You guys have a code for that?'

"We got a code for just about everything. And don't ask if we have a code for stopping at the donut shop, because we don't. I hate the donut jokes because I hate donuts."

"I didn't realize you were so sensitive, Frankie."

"Most of the cops I know are sensitive people, you'd be surprised."

"Come to think of it, the only cop I've ever known well was also a sensitive guy. Maybe too sensitive. Did you know Victor Willis?"

"No, never heard of him. Where did he work?"

"He was everywhere. He was the cop in the Village People."

"Very funny. I was never that sensitive. My brother is the only one who plays that department in our family. I used to think his lifestyle was a great sickness on the human race, but I'm coming to terms with it. Anyway, I hear you doctors have a cure for being gay these days."

The Other Face Of Murder

"Who told you that nonsense?"

"I read it somewhere. Apparently they say you doctors can now cure gayness by putting on a nicotine patch. I heard somewhere that one guy did it and was able to give up having butts for months."

"Hilarious, Frankie. I'm going to find out if Roy is hospitalized. Let me know when you learn more."

THIRTY-SIX

My secretary took only a few minutes to get back to me with Roy's location. An R. Quill was recently admitted to the lockdown psychiatry unit at Good Samaritan Hospital. On the way to the hospital, I rehearsed ways to convey to Roy my support of him. First priority would be to convince him that being committed to a psychiatry ward was nothing to be ashamed of. My father was hospitalized every few years for bipolar disorder, but my mother would never let me visit because they felt mental illness was a stigma, and they were ashamed. When I was younger, she tried to hide his infirmity from me by claiming he had an urgent business meeting in Nebraska or something along those lines.

Glum memories regarding the combination of psychiatric units and family weren't limited to flashbacks concerning father. My cousin, Shoshanna, required mental stabilization on her wedding night not many years ago. She wasn't a fragile person like Roy, but given the particulars of her wedding, nobody was surprised she lost her marbles for a couple weeks.

Shoshanna had married a gentile. They agreed that the wedding would be nondenominational even though she really wanted a Jewish wedding. After some arguments, she convinced her fiancé to at least let the band play a hora. At the wedding dinner, the Jewish guests formed concentric circles and danced around the new couple. The tradition requires the strongest men to lift the bride and groom on chairs as everyone dances around them. Next you lift the parents and other relatives to show them honor. Her father wasn't a very big man, so lifting him was not a problem. However, a much larger Uncle Saul was pretty drunk that night. Unfortunately, he did not hold on to the chair very well. He fell and smashed his skull on the dance floor. Uncle Saul's brain trauma was severe and he died a few minutes after the hora accident. The family visited Shoshanna every day in the psychiatry ward. It was a unique experience for the staff to witness us sitting shiva in a padded room at the facility.

As the elevator doors opened on the third floor of Good Samaritan, my apprehension set in. No longer was I upset that Tarini told Roy, and not me, about her cancer. She was probably doing her best to protect him from ending up in such a place. If only any of us could have better predicted that Grant would emotionally collapse before Roy, but we didn't. It made perfect sense that Roy would wind up in a mental ward after all the disturbing events that had taken place. Given the circumstances of Roy's life, his breakdown wasn't a question of 'if,' but rather a matter of 'when'.

I just hoped his condition was not too severe. These days there is very little funding for the mentally ill, and you have to be pretty unhinged to be admitted to the lockdown unit. At any one moment on a psychiatric ward there is someone who thinks he is Jesus and another person who thinks he's Napoleon. I've always wondered who the psychotics thought they were prior to the times of Napoleon and Jesus.

I picked up the phone outside the Plexiglas door. The nurse at the station behind the door picked up the other end.

"Dr. Weissman here to see patient Quill please."

"What a pleasant surprise, Dr. Weissman," the nurse replied as she buzzed me in.

THIRTY-SEVEN

"Which room is Mr. Quill in?" I asked the charge nurse.

She looked at me kind of funny and said, "She is in number 306."

"When did he get here?"

"She just arrived. I know her very well, given that this is the millionth time she has been admitted, but she is really in a bad way this time."

"She?"

"Yes, she. Who are you looking for, Dr. Weissman?" the charge nurse asked in a direct manner. Her conventional white nurse's uniform topped with a traditional white nurse's hat conveyed a professionalism that has become rare. She looked to be in her sixties, and clearly had seen it all by now, but seemed confused by my question.

"I'm looking for R. Quill."

"Yes, that is Ms. Quill."

"Her first name also starts with an R?"

"Well, yes, you know that because you just asked for R. Quill. Her name is Rachel Quill," the nurse said.

"I'm sorry. I hate how, for privacy's sake, the computers list only the initial letter of psychiatric patients' names. I was actually looking for Roy Quill. He's not here I take it?"

"No, Doctor, but interesting you should ask that."

"Why?"

"Well, that is the name of her son, whom she keeps screaming about. She keeps going on and on, crying how some men came and stole her son today. She won't even eat, and that is unusual for Rachel."

"Really?"

"Yes, she's been very agitated and just keeps yelling how 'they' took her Roy away from her."

"Can I speak with her?"

The nurse started laughing. "Knock yourself out, Doctor. I'm sure you'll get a lot of useful information out of her today."

The nurse pointed to the room and asked, "Do you need me to accompany you?"

"No, thank you," I replied.

"Hello, Ms. Quill. My name is Jerry Weissman. I am a doctor, but I'm also a good friend of Roy's"

She was pacing the room, and ranting, "They are sinners Mr. Wise-man. Every one of them is sinners. They will burn in hell. The fires will be hot for them I tell you."

"Who is 'they,' Ms. Quill?"

She was playing with her hands and looking around the room as if something else was in there with us. "How do I know you're not one of them? You look like you may be one of them."

"One of whom, Ms. Quill?"

She started tugging on her long, unkempt gray hair. Time had been unkind to her. Roy keeps a photo of her in his living room that was taken in her college days. In it she appeared seductive, yet dangerous, like a poppy flower. "I already told the Minister who they are! Why must I repeat myself so many times? I know why you're here. You're here to cast suspicion on my chastity. You think that you are Vishnu, but, young man, you are no Krishna. Roy has sinned, and his friends have paid. He doesn't deserve this and the sun will set him free."

It's been said that even crazy people have motives and reasons for what they say. That's true, but their reasoning is often based on a sea of delusions, which makes the information they are trying to convey useless. That's not to say that delusions can't happen to all of us in times of elevated emotions. I recently had the perception that my friend was murdered in cold blood and that my best friend did it. Fortunately, I was able to discover reality by pursuing my delusions. We can't blame those who have a recurrent illness and are unable to distinguish fantasy from the real world.

"Please, Ms. Quill, if there is anything you can tell me about where Roy is, I can help."

"They have already reported where he is on all three major networks. You should know that, but you are too busy thinking about eating the pussies of black women, aren't you?"

"No, I am not thinking about any such thing. I'm trying to find Roy because I'm worried he is in trouble."

"Oh, he is in trouble, all right. That's why they took him. They took him for trouble. Trouble, trouble, trouble. Double, double, bubble." Her eyeballs rolled upward and she kept repeating, "Trouble, trouble, trouble. Double, double, bubble."

The pressure I felt to find Roy was quickly mounting. My desire to grab his mother by the shirt and shake sense into her was tempered by my own family history. Roy and I shared a bond and a burden. I understood the importance of treating his besieged mother with respect, and that losing my cool would not only be inappropriate, it wouldn't alter outcomes in the slightest.

"Ms. Quill, I can help him, and by doing so, it will help you. But, in order for me to find him, you need to help me. Please, if you know where Roy is, tell me."

She responded immediately. "Like you, I am a spy. However, I am able to transmit incurable disease. It doesn't matter because we still are both patriots for the cause. When you find those that took Roy, you will be rewarded with gold."

"Thank you for speaking with me, Ms. Quill. I will do my best to find Roy and the gold."

THIRTY-EIGHT

Most evenings, there is no greater pleasure than watching the hospital fade in my rearview mirror. Its disappearance usually signifies the end of a long day and a night of relaxation ahead. Watching the hospital vanish after visiting the psychiatric ward, my mood wasn't exactly easy-going. Nothing seemed accomplished by my visit with Ms. Quill, and it made me nervous that precious time had been lost in finding Roy. On the way home I decided to stop by Roy's apartment. His door was unlocked. Inside there were numerous board games scattered on his living room floor. That meant only one thing – that Potter was over last night. I had never met Potter, but I heard Roy talk about him a bunch. He sounded like a pretty strange dude. Roy told me about Potter's unique tattoo. Apparently he has two elephant ears that begin at the base of his organ, making it look like the trunk of an elephant. Sometimes, when he speaks about Potter, it's not clear if he is talking about his best friend or his archenemy. They compete in these late night sci-fi games that I'll never comprehend. A brotherhood of dorkiness binds them together.

I found Roy's Palm Pilot and looked up Potter's phone number. When I got him on the phone, he denied knowing Roy.

"You know him. You were one of the few people he spoke about. Besides, I looked up your number in his Palm Pilot."

"Never heard of him," Potter replied.

"In that case, have you heard of Septimus Mikato-Valkus?"

"A tragic story. Yes, I have."

"Where is he now?"

"Have you not heard of his fate?"

"No. Where is he?"

"He died."

Not again! The ruthlessness of it all walloped me like a hook straight to the temple. That same plague that linked the deaths of Tarini, Grant, and my father had now taken Roy. Sometimes the only thing people have left is a proper goodbye. Not having that final farewell was my living curse. I squeezed the phone so tight I could see my knuckles whiten.

"Died!! How did he die?"

"A tragic story. Not for the faint of heart. Perhaps you should call me when you can handle the news."

"I must know the details now! This is very important."

"It was a dagger to the bowels," Potter said chillingly.

He caught me off guard. "What? Are you serious? Who would stab him?"

"I regretfully report that such information is privileged to the select enlightened few."

"Listen, Potter, or whoever you are, if you don't tell me who stabbed Roy within ten seconds, I will have more Portland cops swarming your place than you can handle."

"Very well then, it was I who delivered his final blow."

"When?" I asked.

"The early hours of the morning."

"Impossible, he was arrested this morning around 8 a.m."

"Inconceivable. He was dead by then, I assure you."

"Fine, then where?"

"In his apartment."

"Bullshit. I'm in his apartment now; there isn't a trace of blood."

Potter thought for a second then replied, "A xenon knife leaves no blood. It is a thousand degrees and coagulates blood vessels as soon as it enters the body. It's a real shame about Septimus. I thought he had a longer fate. The weakness in his character damned him from the beginning. Hopefully he has learned his lessons and will be more successful in the next life."

"You're completely nuts, aren't you? Next life?"

"We start a new tournament round every three months. Sometimes Septimus loses, sometimes he wins. He was the first to be eliminated in this round. He didn't take it well. He was so upset this morning that he threw a glass chalice against the wall.

"You are talking about some Dungeons & Dragons-like fantasy game aren't you?"

"Well, what are you talking about?"

"I'm serious. Roy was arrested around 8 a.m. and now nobody can find him. Do you know where he is?"

"Wow, I thought you were kidding. I don't know where he is. I left his house just after he threw the glass. The dude needs to chill out. It made a pretty loud crash, and then I started freaking out because it was so un-cool. So, we had a short argument with some screaming. Maybe a neighbor called the cops because of the noise."

"Thank you. You are one disturbed person, but you have been helpful."

THIRTY-NINE

Karen and my mother were laughing as they prepared dinner in the kitchen.

"You're so right, Mrs. Weissman, overweight *is* something that just snacks up on you," Karen chuckled. The whimsy one-liner had been so overused by my obese patients that I resented it coming out of her lips.

"Yes, my sweet dear. Well, I am getting in better shape these days. Unfortunately the shape I've chosen is a circle."

Karen stopped laughing when she heard me enter the kitchen. "Did you find Roy?"

"Not yet, but I have some leads. My friend Frankie should be calling me soon with his whereabouts."

Mother, always the optimist, cried out, "He's dead! These things always come in triplets. Poor man, and it must be so hard on his mother."

"Mom, how can you say such a thing? He is a good friend of ours."

"Jerry, if he's not dead then someone else is going to die. I'm telling you, these death waves always come in triplets. I've seen this stuff over and over on Dateline with Stone Philips. If your friend is not dead then I want you and Karen to get out of Portland, so you'll be safely away from the triplet curse. You can both come live with me for a while if you'd like."

"Our jobs are out here, Mother. We aren't going anywhere, and Roy isn't dead, so let's just stop all this crazy talk."

"Crazy? You think your mother is crazy now? What kind of son calls his mother crazy?"

"I didn't call you crazy. I said all this talk is crazy. I saw a crazy mother today, and believe me, you are not crazy. I apologize if you're taking it the wrong way."

Mother opened the oven door and said, "Good. Sit down both of you, because Jerry's crazy mother has baked you an apple kugel that you are going to love."

"Would you like a glass of wine with dinner, Ms. Weissman?" asked Karen.

Mother rarely drinks alcohol. She is one of those people who doesn't get *drunk*, she instead feels *dizzy*. Besides, putting on a happy buzz is not her idea of a good time. Being happy only interferes with her suffering.

"Why Karen darling, that is so sweet of you to offer. I would love a glass of wine."

"Mother! You never drink alcohol."

"I do when there is something to celebrate. Tonight I am celebrating meeting this wonderful woman of yours. Such an angel she is. A real blessing you found each other. I think she is the one for you, Jerry. Treat her like the angel she is, because a strong, pretty woman like her can make many beautiful grandchildren," she said, as she pinched Karen's cheek.

I used to hate when Mother pinched my cheek. In fact, I still hate when she does that. Karen blushed and seemed to cherish the gesture. The whole chummy buddy stuff between Mom and Karen was difficult to grasp, but I was relieved that not only did Mother abstain from crawling up and down Karen's nerves; they actually enjoyed each other's company. Most of my previous girlfriends found her overbearing, and Mother usually looked at them as contestants of sorts. Invariably she had one of two feelings about them – ambiguity or immediate dislike. I thought Karen would fall into the latter category since she isn't Jewish, but miracles seemed to be happening.

Karen appeared to be enjoying the kugel. "You must give me this recipe, Ms. Weissman. I've never had anything like it. You know, Jerry, your mother has been explaining all sorts of fascinating things to me today about Judaism. It's something I simply never knew a lot about. But I'm planning to learn more. There is an introduction to Judaism class at the Jewish Community Center starting next week. I called today, and there was one opening left. Just my luck."

Being in a relationship during happy times is easy, but troublesome times can threaten even a good relationship. Fortunately, in our case, the increased stress was bringing Karen and me closer than before. The stress of recent weeks knocked me into the realization that she was *the* woman for me. No longer was it a matter of desiring her; I truly needed her. Epidemiologic studies show that married men live longer. No surprise to me. I do think love has an anti-aging effect. The rest of my hair would be gray by now, if Karen had not been by my side. I felt grateful that she wanted to learn more about my culture. It indicated a deep interest in who I am and showed devotion to me. However, I never would pressure her to convert to Judaism, unless it was something she really wanted to do for herself and future generations. It's not an easy thing to take on. Maybe the reason we don't believe in hell, is that most Jewish history has already been hell. Israel is the existential hope for the Jews, and even the fate of this small state remains in question. There is only one certainty, that anti-Semitism will forever be a recurrent problem. Being a member of this tiny minority is a burden, and Karen shouldn't feel forced to take on that burden.

I was about to reply to Karen's announcement when my cell phone started ringing. The 702 area code on my caller I.D. was a welcome sight. Las Vegas was on the line.

"Your friend's a wacko," Detective Russo stated.

"Well then, it sounds like you found the right guy," I replied.

"Did you ever figure that this Roy character would try to fight off the police with a toy light-saber? I mean, what the fuck was this dirtball thinking?"

"That doesn't totally surprise me. He's not a dirtball; he's just a bit different."

"So, my buddies said they were just responding to a minor disturbance call for some shouting. However, they ended up needing to apprehend him."

"For fighting them with a toy? That's ridiculous."

"No, son, not for that. They were about to let him go on a warning, but they ran his name on the computer, and the guy has a warrant."

"A warrant? Roy? You've got to be kidding me. He smokes weed every now and then, but he is not a criminal."

"Consider explaining that to some really pissed off cop in Tillamook. He apparently is wanted for defacing police station property."

"Are you frickin' kidding me, Frankie? He pooped in the crapper and clogged up the toilet. That's it. He just recently told me the entire story. There is no way that he ever did anything more to that police station."

"Clogged a toilet? Jeez, my colleagues told me the Tillamook cop was really ticked off at your friend. This Tillamook cop, named Officer Sperelakis, even drove all the way to Portland to pick Roy up. Sometimes there's no janitorial staff in those small town stations, but it seems a little overboard to be so upset about clogging the toilet. Besides, that's not the entire story."

"What do you mean, Frankie?"

"When Sperelakis picked your friend up from the Portland station, he also told my boys that he's charging your friend with methamphetamine distribution. He said he just hadn't had enough time to put the warrant out yet. He said he has the evidence back in Tillamook with Roy's fingerprints all over the bags of drugs. Your friend is looking down the barrel of some hard time."

The boiling rage in my veins felt thick like molten lava. "That is total bullshit! There is no way in this universe he would ever do meth, and he sure as hell would be too nervous to ever sell drugs. He's being framed. This crooked cop is setting up an innocent man over a goddamned clogged toilet!"

"O.K. Just calm down. My friends in Portland also thought this was a little suspicious. We all know what meth addicts look like, and they told me your friend did not look like some junkie. He sounds a bit weird, but apparently he's no junkie. My buddies also thought it was strange that another officer didn't mention anything about narcotics trafficking until he took custody of Roy. They tell me this Sperelakis guy has a reputation for being a hothead. So, I believe you, Doc."

"You don't understand, Frankie. This is a man with mental illness in his family," I started saying.

"Hey, I can relate. You've seen my brother. The guy's a disturbed psycho."

I started pleading with him. "Roy won't make it two days in jail. He's fragile. We need to get him out."

"Hey, a favor for a favor is what I promised you, Doc. I uphold my end of every bargain. I'm pulling into the Vegas airport now and I'll be at PDX around ten tonight. Pick me up, and bring some help, because this may get ugly."

"What are we going to do?"

"We are going to Tillamook to get your friend, hopefully before he sustains any bodily injury. I'm sick and tired of these crooked cops giving the rest of us a bad name. We are going down there to teach that cocksucker a lesson."

"Seriously? We're going to rough-up a cop? Are you crazy?"

"Hey, it won't be the first police station I've turned honest. Now you listen to me, son. Men are like turtles. We only get things done by sticking our necks out once in a while. It's payback time. I'm excited about this. It's getting so damn boring out in Vegas, I can't even tell you. It's time for some more action in my life. I'll see ya tonight."

FORTY

Meanwhile, at the jailhouse in Tillamook…

Roy finished cleaning the toilet with Ajax and a toothbrush. These were the only tools Officer Sperelakis allowed him to have. That wouldn't have been so bad if it were only the outside of the toilet he was forced to clean. Roy was also forced to clean the entire inner bowl of the toilet without rubber gloves. There was no way for him to reach into the bottom of the bowl without submerging his hand and arm in the water. Officer Sperelakis took a piss in the toilet just before Roy started cleaning it. He told Roy that he couldn't flush the toilet until he was done scrubbing, or the rest of the job would be done entirely with his tongue.

"Don't I get one phone call?" Roy asked submissively.

Sperelakis answered, "You don't get it, boy, do you? You ain't even under arrest yet. You are my prisoner. The arresting part comes later. I just pray you will give me a good struggle to justify my actions."

"I need to get out of here, sir. My mother's in the hospital."

"Well ain't that just perfect. Because that's exactly where ya gonna end up when this is all through. Maybe you and your momma can share a hospital bed and save some money." Officer Sperelakis cracked his chewing gum threateningly.

"P-p-please sir, I am so sorry for clogging your toilet. I've cleaned it just as you asked." "You sure it's clean?"

"Yes. It's clean."

Officer Sperelakis was tapping his nightstick against the sole of his shoe when he asked, "clean enough to shower in?"

"Nobody showers in the toilet, sir."

"Well I guess there's always a first, ain't there?" With that he grabbed Roy's ponytail and stuffed his face in the urine for about ten seconds before flushing the toilet with Roy's head still submerged.

FORTY-ONE

When I called Earl to tell him Roy had been arrested, his reaction mirrored mine.

"Ain't that the berries? I'm with your amigo Frankie; we're getting that boy out of jail tonight."

"So we are just going to bust into the cop station and free him?" I asked.

"Come on, we are talking about our boy Roy! There are those that kick butt, and those that kiss butt. I, for one, do not fall into the latter category. Savvy planning is the key. Let's go get some costumes before we pick up our Las Vegas connection from the airport. There could be surveillance cameras at the cop station, and the Oregon State Medical Board won't look kindly on this if we get noticed."

"You're telling me? I'm shocked we have our licenses at all after the past few weeks. Who should we disguise ourselves as?"

Earl pondered for a moment, "I think I have the perfect answer for our buddy Roy. We have to be Star Wars characters. Can you imagine the look on his face when members of the *Rebellion* bust in to save him? Oh, it's going to be awesome! We'll meet at the costume store at Washington Square Mall in twenty minutes."

Reality will defeat well intentioned fantasies, but I had to admit the plan sounded glorious.

At the store, Earl put on an Ewok costume. It seemed ironic that big Earl was dressing as an Ewok. In the movie they were small teddy-bear like characters. The entire outfit was covered with fake brown fur, including the mask. He looked more like a grizzly. He checked himself out in the mirror and seemed pleased.

"Well, see there Jerry, don't I look cuter than a sack full of puppies?"

"No doubt, let me give you a hug, you adorable thing," I said, as I wrapped my arms around his pudgy belly. There was a faint odor of McTarnahans Ale on his breath

"Back off you fairy ass-munching drama queen."

"Oh, come on, Earl, enjoy a little loving. Besides, there's a good chance we'll be in the jailhouse for a while after tonight. You should feel honored by my affections. Guys like me are prize possessions in the slammer."

"Seriously, Jerry, you better stop trying to put your crankshaft in my caboose. Now get your god-damn hands off of me, you hemorrhoid hit man." If there is one thing most Southern men don't joke about, it's a man showing affection to another man, even if it's done in a playful manner.

I let go of my furry friend and suggested a costume exchange. "I think you'd be much better suited as a character that is supposed to be taller than a meter. Try on a Chewbacca costume."

"I already asked the manager before you arrived. They are plain out of Wookiee attire. In fact they only have three other Star Wars characters left. One of the costumes we can't wear. That's a Darth Vader, because he was on the dark side of the force. We want the *Rebellion* to free our boy, and we should remain true to character for Roy's sake. We need to make sufficient with the merchandise they have left."

"Well, what's left?"

"There is a Yoda, which we should give to our Vegas connection. There is also a Princess Leia, which you'll have to wear."

"Screw that, I'm not wearing a Princess Leia costume."

Earl had never been plagued by an inferiority complex, and it ticked me off when he tried to inflict one on me.

"Jerry, you have to be the damn Princess. We can't expect Russo to be in drag. Self-respecting cops don't go there."

"Forget it, Earl. I'll just be the Cat in the Hat or something."

"Dammit, you can't start this crap now! This isn't about me or you. This here is about Roy. You've got to do it for Roy. Think about that poor sissy boy and all he's gone through. If you don't go as a Princess, then I'm bailing out of this whole thing. Either fish or cut bait."

Earl was acting that way to get back at me. As he limped around the store, I realized that I did owe him whatever would make him happy. He would never let me forget the night I dressed up as

Princess Leia, but it had to be done. Besides, Roy really would be appreciative of our efforts. The two things Roy fantasized about most were Star Wars and 'Latino chicks'. Going in drag as a Latino woman was far from a consideration, so Princess Leia it was.

FORTY-TWO

On the way to the airport Earl and I had our final conversation about the night of Tarini's death. The reason for her being in the pantry still puzzled me and Karen. Earl, as always, had an explanation.

"I hesitated for a few seconds prior to the injection, but eventually reasoned that a better time may not present itself. After administering the Vecuronium, we both kept vigil at the bedside. I reckon that her pulse stopped about nine minutes later. The entire thing was peaceful. Very similar to the experience of taking my dog Gunner to the vet when he was put to sleep. Not that Tarini was anything like a pet, but you know what I'm saying. Anyway, we let her rest for a few minutes while Grant wept quietly on her chest. Gave it a while to let her soul make its way to heaven.

"Grant and I decided to take her home, so nobody else would be involved. It would have been easy to unload her there in his garage and then put her in her own bed. I would spend the rest of the night with Grant and the body, and we would report her death in the morning. When you got up and didn't find us there, you would just figure we had decided to leave early. We would explain to you later that Tarini had become ill and asked us to take her home. In retrospect, we definitely should have left her body right there where she died. It wouldn't have raised so many questions. But who thinks logically in that kind of situation?"

"As if you think logically in most situations?"

"As if your jokes will ever be funny in any situation?"

"Point conceded. So, what happened?"

"I carried her up the stairs. My head was dizzy from the booze, lack of sleep, and hauling her up those stairs. Damn near passed out on those stairs. Needing rest, I stopped off at your kitchen prior to carrying her to my truck. I was going to get a quick drink of water, pull my truck into your garage so a neighbor wouldn't witness the loading, then drive away, with Grant behind me in his car. Honest to God that was my intent, but the pantry door was ajar with an open bag of Oreo cookies resting on the shelf..."

That had always been Earl's kryptonite – Oreo cookies. I knew exactly where the inconceivable story was heading. Of all the outlandish, cockamamie, idiotic things that could screw plans up after euthanizing a friend – Oreo cookies.

I chastised him. "Are you for real?"

"I know it. I should have put Tarini down first, but my stomach got the best of me. While reaching out for a cookie, I lost my balance and we fell square into the shelves. Them shelves must be made of toothpicks, because they busted apart like thin plywood. I was irate as a hornet. Not only did I cause a loud ruckus, my pants were soaked with salsa. In a panic, I ran downstairs to get my pants off, and then tried to explain the situation to Grant. A bit cranky about the blunder, he pushed and smacked me up the stairs. He wouldn't let me change into the extra pair of scrub pants I had in my bag. That's why I was in boxer shorts. When we got back to the pantry, there you were. Smack dab involved in the whole mess. Maybe we should have made clean of the entire situation, but hindsight is 20/20."

Frankie's flight arrived a few minutes early. When we got to PDX he was smoking a cigarette on the curb outside baggage claim. He had a brown leathery tan and wore a stylish dark-blue custom tailored suit. A narrow awning that extended over the curb provided some shelter from the drenching sky.

Before climbing into the car, he stared through the window at the humongous Ewok and transvestite Princess Leia, but didn't mention them right away. Frankie said he was pleased to be back in Oregon, but there was the serious look of business on his face. With each drag of the cigarette, he appeared to be solidifying his plan for the night. His thinning hair was matted from the moisture which falsely made it appear that he had used hair gel.

After hearing our explanation for the costumes, Frankie refused his, and said, "Hey, I think it's a good idea for you two. No reason anyone needs to know your identity. As far as I'm concerned, I want this guy to know exactly who he is dealing with when it comes to me. I'm going to teach this potzo piece of garbage a lesson. Just here to straighten things out."

To us, Frankie was the real Clint Eastwood. He was aged with skin of wrinkled concrete, but more of a badass than any bodybuilder there ever was. He always talked as if what he said was the final word. No room for negotiation at his table. The man commanded respect and his aura of authority had no amateur mannerisms. Intimate conversation was never required to know who the true Frankie was. I had only met him once before the airport, but even then it was obvious, you don't fuck around with Frankie Russo.

"Sounds good to me Frankie," I said. "I'll pull over and get the Yoda costume out of the trunk so I can wear it."

Earl was totally opposed. "Listen, cupcake, we don't have time. It took us long enough to get these costumes on. We need to get Roy out of jail ASAP. No more monkeying around with this other stuff. You just keep on driving until we hit Tillamook."

Frankie said, "He's right, we need to get a move on this journey. Besides, my lady, you look just fine."

FORTY-THREE

The ride out to Tillamook started in an unpleasant manner. Earl kept releasing gas that smelled like burnt cheese. Even his copious application of Old Spice deodorant wasn't adequately masking the stench. I was the driver, because I never let Earl drive my car. He learned to drive on a John Deere, and it showed. Actually he's never driven a car. He's owned a succession of three different colossal pickup trucks since he got his license. At a four-way stop, he believes that the vehicle with the largest tires has the right of way. He's also the kind of driver who thinks road signs are only mere gimmicks for older drivers who crave structured routine.

I noticed Earl had his black leather bag with him. "Why did you bring your medical bag with you?" I inquired.

"You never know when somebody might get sick. Someone could shoot you in the leg, just like that, out of nowhere," he said with a snap of his fingers. "Besides, honeybee, you might get your period at any time, so I decided to bring some pain killers."

Earl and Frankie were as calm as could be, while I worried that my last night of freedom was being spent in my vehicle being hot-boxed by Earl's pungent odors. Earl sensed my fear and decided to call me on it.

"Girl, you look as nervous as a whore in church."

Anger among friends has an expiration date. Sometimes the shelf life can be years. Fortunately, Earl didn't hold a grudge against me for too long despite the gunshot wounds and all. Nevertheless, he had his frustrations with me, and they were being manifested.

"I'm not a girl, and I'm doing just fine."

"Peaches, you look like someone put a quiver in your liver."

"I'm fine. Will you stop the crap?" Being dressed as a woman wasn't all that humiliating. I just was annoyed that Earl got so elated about it. I've been in much more embarrassing situations many times in my life. Even as a youngster in a Wisconsin summer camp I experienced more upsetting experiences. There was the day we were on the floating raft in the middle of the lake. My counselor pulled off the swim trunks of both me and my friend Jim. Then the whistle was blown, a signal that called everyone to the beach for 'head count'. The senior camp staff took the 'head counts' seriously as a safety measure. If you weren't on the beach by the time the second whistle blew in three minutes, you cleaned the camp cafeteria. Not being at 'head count' by the third whistle, resulted in no swimming for a week, and you cleaned the cafeteria everyday for a week. Jim and I decided to go up on the beach for 'head count' despite being naked. The counselors were all laughing at us, as were the many boys.

Earl kept egging me on. "What are you so upset about, Barbie? Everything is going to be just fine. You do, however, need to drive a little faster so we get there before sunrise. Just relax. Let's sing some songs."

With that, Earl and Frankie started singing along with the radio. It was Bob Dylan singing *Like a Rolling Stone*:

> You're invisible now; you got no secrets to conceal. How does it feel to be on your own?

Despite their urging, I refused to sing along. Most Jews I know have lousy voices. Bob Dylan exemplifies that. Maybe that's why we don't have choirs during our services. We can't find that many people in the congregation who can sing well. Instead, we have a cantor who is the one person designated to do the singing during our services.

Earl stopped singing, and said, "Lady, what the hell are you so afraid of? This is how bad cops get their small town justice all the time. Trust me; I grew up in a small town. We don't take kindly to injustice. It doesn't matter if you are the police or the minister. Treat people with respect, and you'll be respected. Treat people like dirt, and your face ought to be in the dirt. We'll give this cop a chance. He can cooperate if he wants, or else it will be fist city."

Was it coincidental that Earl had such a disciplinary attitude being from a town called Reform, Alabama? Guys from towns like Reform seem so physical when it comes to forcing behavioral changes. Perhaps it's because they grow up on farms and have to strong-arm animals. The Horse Whisperer philosophy hadn't yet taken hold in places like Reform. Earl acknowledged modern justice to be only a philosophy worth considering. He once told me that telling the judge, *your Honor, the man had conduct that seriously called for some killin'*, periodically worked as a valid defense in his hometown.

"I mean no disrespect, Doc, but your friend is right," stated Frankie. "It isn't like the big cities. There isn't a news investigation or a firing by the mayor. If you are sure you're fighting the good fight, then you have to take matters into your own hands in these situations. We'll be the dignified cats, but if this guy provokes the kitty too much, then the kitty will become a lion."

I still wasn't convinced. "So let me get this straight one more time. We are just going to walk into the cop station and demand that Roy be released?"

Frankie replied, "Son, sure as night is dark, that's the plan."

Inside me, everything felt unsettled, off-balance. My sense of puzzlement hadn't been that strong since college. College did confuse me, and therefore education did its intended job. After growing up in a traditional home, learning a plethora of different opinions was an un-grounding experience. Medical school did its job at re-grounding. Facts and strictly following the guidance of senior physicians was the only way, or it was the highway. That night, Earl and Frankie were also teaching me a curriculum they had learned by experience. There weren't, however, any other smart alternatives that I could think of. A jury trial for Roy could take years and perchance end in a wrongful conviction. At that moment, I realized my trust and loyalty towards Earl had been restored. Regaining confidence had nothing to do with him, and everything to do with me. Learning how to trust again is no easy task. In only a few hours, the biggest mistake, or possibly the most heroic event in my life would transpire. For some reason, my faith that we were heading down the road in the right direction strengthened. Father always said, *sometimes in life you just got to get up and walk the tightrope.*

We were halfway to Tillamook when my phone rang.

"Bubelah, where are you?" I wouldn't have answered had I known it was my mom. Since she was calling from my house, my cell phone didn't give its special warning ring.

"I'm in a car with some friends. Go to sleep, Mother, I'll be home later."

"Later? It's almost midnight. I've been so worried. It's to the point that I'm worried about my worrying."

"I'm helping my friends on some errands, I'll be home soon."

"How soon? Where is it you're going?" Any time there is the slightest uncertainty, her thoughts become dominated by all the conceivable disasters that could be happening.

"Very soon, Mother. Just go to sleep and we'll have a nice breakfast in the morning."

"I can't even think about breakfast, my heartburn is so horrible right now. Your poor mother comes out to visit you, and my son, the doctor, spends the entire night out doing shenanigans? I need this torment like I need a hole in my head. Tonight is the Sabbath, Jerry, the blessed Sabbath."

"Mother, don't you want me to help out my friend in need? I'm a doctor. I help people out in bad situations. You need to respect that." While the details weren't something she needed to know, I didn't want to lie to her either. I've never made a good liar because my memory is not that reliable for false facts. A good liar must remember exactly what he lied about to get away with it. When does a half-truth become a full lie? When I'm the one trying to present a half-truth to Mother.

"Jerry, what are you saying? Are you calling me a nuisance? Fine, I'll just sit here in the dark with my heartburn. I don't want to be a nuisance to anybody."

Frankie grabbed the phone out of my hand. He started talking to my mother, but I couldn't hear her responses.

"Yes, Ms. Weissman, he is really helping some people out tonight...

That's right; undeniably, he is a blessing to the community...

Yes, he is being very safe...

That's why he gave me the phone so he could concentrate on the road...

Ms. Weissman, I'll make sure he gets home safe...

You're right, it's getting late and he shouldn't drive, so we'll get a taxi...

You're right, taxis are too expensive, and so we'll take the bus...

Understood, you're right; buses aren't safe at this hour...

O.K. we'll call you if we need a ride. Nice talking to you too."

Frankie hung up and said, "Sounds like a very nice lady. You should be proud to have such a caring mother. If only everybody were raised with such affection, we wouldn't have all these despicable criminals."

FORTY-FOUR

Halfway through the drive, both Frankie and Earl fell asleep. Long drives have always been my time for contemplation. Apprehensive about our arrival in Tillamook, I recalled Martin Luther King's words: *A man who won't die for something is not fit to live.* The thought put me at ease. We may have been about to get into serious trouble, but there was no question we were doing the right thing.

Finally, I found myself with a long stretch of time to think about the last few weeks. I had become somewhat less judgmental about what Earl and Grant had done for Tarini, although certain questions seemed more complicated. Were they heroic in what they'd done? As a society, we do, on occasion, celebrate suicide as heroic. If a soldier throws himself on a grenade to save his friends, he's a hero. If you step in front of a bullet aimed for the President, you'll make the secret service hall of fame. Tarini's fate had been one of severe disability and death. Since the tumor involved her most vital organ, it would have ultimately stolen her intelligence and spirit. She preferred to jump in front of the bullet rather than lose her Commander-in-Chief. Losing a baby hadn't broken her faith in the future, but a Glioblastoma did.

Both sides of the assisted suicide controversy had been tugging furiously at me. Like an atom splitting apart, my conscience contained explosive energy pertaining to the subject. As a healer, my role in caring for the dying became entangled in convoluted derangement. Divorcing dogma to discover the virtues of alternative viewpoints never comes easily. Trying to make rules about assisted suicide is difficult, if not impossible. Was there a need to judge on a case by case basis? On the other hand, if there are no hard rules, how does one proceed in the task of reaching an ethical, moral resolution?

I reflected on the death of my most recent patient. Her daughter had tried to do the right thing for her mother, which resulted in the painful consequences that most hospitalized Americans will suffer at the end of their lives. Her mother died with a tube in her bladder to allow urination, a tube in her throat to breathe, a tube in her stomach to feed, multiple tubes in her veins for medicines, and a balloon in an

The Other Face Of Murder

artery to circulate blood. While there can be dignity in a vigorous fight against death, there is no dignity in that kind of fight. People allow family members to go through such torture, sometimes in the belief of miracles. The media also spins modern medicine as the new era of miracles - even though we never have kept a human alive forever. People understandably have an awful time facing the reality of death, and certainly there is a strong argument that delusional positive thinking is often essential for survival. I've witnessed many patients who refused to give in to their diseases, and they survived a bit longer as a result. However, there can come a time when unrealistic thinking no longer assists survival, but rather results in mental and physical torture for patients and families. Perceptions do often obscure reality.

Doctor Ira Byock, a modern leader in hospice and palliative medicine, has said that *good deaths were not random events or matters of luck; they could be understood and, perhaps, fostered.* That revelation escapes too many physicians and families. It was a revelation that Grant and Earl had, and a revelation that I eventually had. I knew that my practice patterns would be forever changed. No longer would my purpose as a doctor be focused solely on curing and prolonging life. Quality of life would take on as much importance as quantity.

I reflected on grief, anger, and guilt. It's not that Grant had done anything evil by turning his self-loathing inward. I just wish Grant had released some of his negative energy on me. He should have screamed at me for not trusting him and Earl. My buffoonery only complicated his ability to cope with a personal tragedy.

How did I miss the real tragedy during the entire time I was trying to solve the mystery of Tarini's death? If I had put more effort into helping Grant instead of trying to incriminate him, there may have been a different outcome. I hoped, in the future, to overcome the culpability I felt about Grant's death, but at that moment there was only self animosity.

Another thought crossed my mind: Concentrate on staying awake while driving or there would be three more deaths to add to the list of tragedies in the world.

FORTY-FIVE

We pulled into Tillamook very early in the morning. An empty feeling of loneliness was settling in, and it was nice to have an excuse to wake up the boys. Driving solo into the desolate wee hours alters moods. The mind can play tricks on you, and even elicit some paranoia. My tired brain was losing confidence. Frankie and Earl were still in the car, but for some reason I started to suspect that the only thing willing to accompany me in getting Roy out of jail would be my shadow. Exhaustion was making me lose faith in others. Repressed assumptions were again unveiling themselves.

The Truth or Consequences Church of Christ caught my eye as we traveled the main road, and we continued on until we arrived at police headquarters. There hadn't been a vehicle on the road, other than mine. After exiting the car, we all paused for a moment outside the front door of the police station. My legs felt weak, and I wanted to lean against the red brick structure that resembled an old school house. Frankie cleared his smoky throat, opened the door, and we followed him in.

We found our soon-to-be victim asleep on a couch next to his desk. Frankie went over and tapped him on the shoulder to wake him up. He sat up in a startled manner, pretending that he wasn't asleep. Roy sat on the cot in his locked cell, his knees bent, and his arms wrapped around his legs. When he looked up at the Ewok and Princess Leia, the costumes did appear to have the intended effect that Earl hoped for. His skin went pale and his eyes didn't blink for the next several minutes.

"I'm Officer Sperelakis, and who in God's name are you weirdoes?"

Frankie did all the talking. He is one of those guys who means every word he says, and Sperelakis immediately seemed to respect that. "The name is Russo. Frankie Russo. Sheriff for the Portland PD," he said, as he showed him his badge. Frankie began to wag his index finger in the air as he explained, "We didn't come here for any trouble. We are here to take Roy Quill back to Portland."

Officer Sperelakis was angered, his face flushed, and he asked, "What's with the freak outfits?"

"These are two of my colleagues. Let's just say they are doing some undercover work tonight," Frankie replied, and then inhaled a deep breath to gather his strength and composure.

"Sheriff Russo you say? Well, old-timer, you know you have no jurisdiction to come into my town and demand the release of my prisoner. Take it up with the Tillamook county judge later today if you have a problem with that. We have a very fair judge who is always willing to dispense justice. I should know since he's my cousin."

Frankie got right in his face and told him, "I have moral jurisdiction, asshole! That boy is innocent. You set him up. You let him go this minute, or you'll be paying a penalty with the state District Attorney, me, and the press later today."

They stared each other down like two junkyard dogs that had come across a fresh bone. The cop reached for his holster, but Frankie gave him a swift jab to the mouth before Sperelakis could get his hand on his gun. Frankie disarmed him before he even had another chance to think.

Earl screamed out in joy, "That's my man, Russo! You kill it, and I'll grill it."

The skin on two of Frankie's knuckles had split open. His knuckle lacerations weren't nearly as big as the open gash Sperelakis had in his middle upper lip. The gash extended to the base of the nasal septum. The punch made him appear as if he were born with a cleft palate, like those third world children that Operation Smile goes around the globe fixing. He tried talking, but it became clear that not only was he stunned, his front teeth were no longer aligned. The rapidly swelling flesh of his tongue, which he nearly bit through, promptly changed his ability to articulate. His blood-splattered, well-pressed, khaki patrolman shirt resembled a Jackson Pollock canvas.

We found the cell keys, and released Roy, who was never happier until the day they announced the Battlestar Galactica Box Set would be released on DVD. He ran over to the cop's desk and emptied out a drawer full of wrist watches. I guess Officer Sperelakis must have had some weird fetish about keeping the watches of his prisoners. Roy found his gold watch and threw it to me.

"It's a 24 karat antique. My daddy left it in his will for me. I can't wear it anymore. It will bring back too many memories of this entire thing. You take it. When I see you wearing it, that watch will symbolize the friendship and courage you all demonstrated for me tonight. May the force stay with you."

The watch battery had died, but it's something I didn't consider replacing. Even a broken watch will provide the correct time twice a day, and that was good enough for me. The usefulness of that watch had nothing to do with keeping time. It conjured up memories.

"You know, I saw your mom yesterday at the hospital. She told me when I found you that I'd be rewarded with gold." Sometimes life is about what you get, and other times it's about what you give. That was a night I both gave and received.

Roy didn't seem surprised about his mother. "She has her strange side, but her predictions always seem to come true."

Earl escorted the half-dazed Sperelakis to my car. I hadn't been planning to kidnap anybody that night, but things at the time seemed to be going all right, so I never stopped to ask any questions. On we went, at the mercy of the universe.

FORTY-SIX

As we pulled into the parking lot behind the church, Frankie was lecturing Sperelakis about how cops need to take the ethical high ground. He told him that modern men need to start acting with respect again. Frankie blamed the media and the current role models for America's declining values, and said we needed heroes like Joe DiMaggio to resurface.

A large fluorescent sign advertised the hours of church worship. In smaller letters underneath the hours it also read, *Free Trip to Heaven, Details Inside!* Earl shook his head in pity, and turned to Officer Sperelakis to say, "Well too bad for you we won't be going inside. I guess this isn't the night you'll make it to heaven. Unfortunately for you, there is an alternative to heaven that you will experience. Yes, my friend, you're going to end up a little *south* of heaven tonight. Lucky for you, you'll have a true gentleman, one who knows the South, to be your guide." He then pulled out the Z-FORCE 100,000V stun gun he had confiscated from me at his house. Earl explained to the cop that he would have to follow all directions perfectly, or he would "experience the shocker".

Frankie lit a cigarette while stating matter-of-factly, "I'll wait in the car with Roy. You two enjoy yourselves."

As Earl exited the car, he said, "You got it Frankie. We'll be back quicker'n a greased pig." Earl went to the trunk and pulled out the Yoda outfit from the large plastic store bag. Next, he then pulled out a Chewbacca costume from the same bag.

"I thought you said they were all out of Wookiee costumes? What gives?" I asked, as a chilly morning coastal breeze cut though the flimsy fabric of my Leia garb. If anybody needed the warm furry apparel, it was me.

"Relax, bitch. They were out of Wookiee costumes after I bought the last one, just before you arrived at the store. I knew we'd need it for this very important chunk of the mission."

Earl proceeded to cut a hole in the buttocks section of the Wookiee costume with the trauma scissors he had in his medical bag.

I feared the worst was about to happen. He then ordered Officer Sperelakis to strip naked and then dress himself in the costume, which happened to fit perfectly. There was no way I would let Earl sodomize that man, and I was quite verbal about letting him know that. I told Earl that he had caused the death of enough people in the last few weeks by sticking things up their ass.

"Relax, Ms. Worrywart," he replied. "You Northern girls have watched *Deliverance* a few too many times. Trust me; I want nothing to do with another dude's asshole. You need to chill out. You're acting like a long-tailed cat in a room full of rocking chairs. I'm not the kind of guy that would break open another dude's be-hymen."

Earl led us to a large iron crucifix placed a few feet from the back entrance of the church. The gargantuan Ewok was hobbling along on his wounded leg, carrying the stun gun in his right hand, and his medical bag in the left.

I adamantly reaffirmed my opinion to Earl that, "We aren't sodomizing him and we are not torturing anybody. Besides there's nothing more we need from him. Let's just get out of here."

Soon we were all standing in front of the five-foot cross. Earl started to duct tape Officer Sperelakis' hands to the horizontal bar of the cross and said, "This has nothing to do with torture. Attitude adjustment is what we will humbly partake in tonight. Purely, a lesson in learning to see things from another perspective. If you don't like it, then send my name to the Geneva Convention, whenever that stupid thing is held next. Anyway, if you think what I'm about to do is torture, then go ahead and feel sorry for me, but don't feel sorry for this dickhead."

"Why would I feel sorry for you?"

As the Wookiee stood crucified in front of us, Earl explained, "Any psychiatrist will tell you that it's the tortured souls that turn into the torturers. So, go ahead and pray for my tortured soul. Besides, Officer Sperelakis here is about to be freed. He's going to tell the truth, and the truth shall set his soul free. The only deeds we will partake in tonight will be for his own good. We aren't going to hurt anything but his pride."

He then pulled out from his medical bag a nasal-gastric tube and lubricated it with a packet of sterile Surgilube. A nasal-gastric tube is a common, small diameter, rubber tube we put in patients stomachs via their noses to feed them when they lose their ability to swallow effectively. Then, with perfect technique, he placed the tube through the breathing hole in the Wookiee costume into the left nostril of Officer Sperelakis, and quickly advanced the tube through the esophagus into the stomach while his victim gagged. About a foot of the tube was appropriately left hanging out of the Wookiee nose.

Earl pulled out a Dictaphone that he used for transcriptions at his office. He pressed Record, and said, "This is an oral history of Officer Sperelakis recounting his sins. Since the priest has retired for the evening, I've decided I'd be willing to hear his confession at church tonight. It's now time for my first question of the evening. What charges were you planning to bring Roy Quill up on?"

Each time the officer denied wrong doing, Earl poured more Syrup of Ipecac down the nasal-gastric tube. Ipecac is a plant extract that is very irritating to the stomach. It is used by medical professionals to induce instant vomiting when children accidentally ingest a poison. Sperelakis was vomiting and dry-heaving so much at one point, that he probably couldn't have gotten the words out for a spoken confession. Between vomiting he would just plead with us saying, "Please…stop…please." He did eventually start to cry.

An infraction of our oath to Hippocrates of *first do no harm* was definitely taking place, but I felt there was little moral ground for me to lecture Earl on. With vengeance on my mind, I had recently broken into Earl's house and discharged a round of ammunition into his leg. Besides, talking a man out of rendering revenge can be a hard thing to do. This was Earl's turn for dispensing retribution.

Earl didn't show any sympathy. He seemed to be displaying about as much self-control as an eighteen year-old male virgin would at a strip-club while drunk and tripping on ecstasy with three credit cards in his pocket. "It's time to get off the pity-pot and start living life like a man. Let me make something clear to you, Mr. Policeman. Today is your day of reckoning. Wash away your sins. The sooner you do it, the easier it will be for all of us. You know what? I just remembered, it's Saturday morning. We can keep at this all weekend since I don't need to be back at the office until Monday." He showed the petrified cop that he still had about a dozen bottles of Ipecac in his medical bag. A putrid foul stink was being emitted from the vomit all over the Wookiee fur.

Officer Sperelakis finally gave in. "O.K. I tried to set him up on a methamphetamine charge!"

Earl was only partly satisfied. "We need details. The devil is in the details. Confess your sins completely, or face damnation."

"I busted a speeder on the highway the other morning and found the drugs in his car. While I was arresting the man, I got a call over the radio that they had your friend in custody. I let the smuggler go and kept the drugs with the intent of setting your friend up."

"You've done a great job tonight. You should be proud of yourself. Confession can really ease the mind." He pressed stop on the Dictaphone.

After the confession, Earl was kind enough to pour some Compazine, an anti-nausea medication, down the nasal-gastric tube to inhibit further vomiting. I was pleased to see him taking some mercy on the man. That was until I realized the reason why Earl had cut a hole in the ass of the costume. It was an escape route for a whole bunch more shit to come. Earl poured a large bottle of Lactulose down the tube. Lactulose is a powerful laxative used in hospitals, and he put about ten times the normal dose down the tube. He then yanked the tube out of the Wookiee. Earl proceeded to pull out a large, bright pink, glow-in-the-dark, strap-on dildo from the bottom of his doctor's bag. "Come on, man," I said, "you agreed, no sodomy."

Earls rolled his eyes at me through the Ewok mask with disbelief. It was obvious that he had strategically planned this all in advance, and was offended that I wasn't enthusiastically impressed with his masterful scheme. He strapped on the dildo around the Wookiee's waist.

Earl's last words at the scene were a straightforward, "All right. Let's go."

I stared at the tragic Chewbacca figure that was strapped to a crucifix, with vomit all over his fur, ass cheeks exposed, and a bright pink dildo hanging off the crotch area. In less than an hour the laxatives would start working. There would be no long term physical damage, but he would have some pretty strong memories of that night. Discovering the scene sure was going to be disturbing to some people come daylight.

FORTY-SEVEN

We got on the road back to Portland. Some have said that the darkest hour is right before the dawn. Pulling into Tillamook had aroused in me a sense of panic, but leaving was pure bliss. As we passed the city of Hillsboro, the sun started to rise. Being early Saturday morning, most of the traffic was heading in the opposite direction. The weekend warriors were heading for the coast. A well-earned truism is that *it's a frequent sight in Oregon to see five-thousand dollar mountain bikes on the roof racks above cars of far lesser value.*

There was a sharp bend in the road that I almost missed because of inattention to the signs. The close call struck me as metaphorical. The importance of being willing to make consequential turns as we continue this journey through life can't be understated. Tarini's death and Roy's arrest and rescue were more than enough to spark a re-evaluation of my past and to modify the path ahead.

I've realized that the strengths and weaknesses of every person are revealed only through time and experience. Even when it comes to death - never squander a tragedy; learn from it. Remember the warning signs you missed, and then become enriched by the misery. That's what's required in becoming a good doctor or friend or son or whatever. Otherwise, the future will be paralyzed by fear.

As we continued on the road home, Earl and Frankie slept, and Roy played an eerily appropriate Alanis Morissette CD about the human plight:

> *You love you learn*
> *You cry you learn*
> *You lose you learn*

"When did Tarini tell you about the brain cancer?" I asked.

"Is that really what she had? Jeez, I always thought so," Roy replied.

"What do you mean you thought so? You knew so. You left it on my answering machine that she had brain cancer."

Roy acted astonished. "I really did think that's what she had, but it was only a hunch. She never told me anything about cancer."

"Ohhh great. That's just great. I should do a gene study on you and your mother. Perhaps I'll win the Nobel Prize for finding the psychic gene."

Foreseeing the future must be both a blessing and a curse. The constant obligation of striving to change bad things before they happened would be an overwhelming responsibility. Particularly, knowing a friend had cancer before they did would be extraordinarily cruel.

Roy, as if reading my thoughts, said, "I should have told Tarini to get it checked out the second it popped in my mind."

Guilt can be so irrational, because it stems from unrealistic expectations within you or placed on you by another. Growing up with my mother has made me an expert in the field. Even after my mother dies, I will have accrued enough self-condemnation to subsist off the dividends. In fact, I feel guilty just for even thinking that someday my mother will die.

I told Roy, "It's not like you gave her cancer. As a doctor I'm telling you there was no way to cure her cancer. Don't be burdened by something you couldn't help, all right?"

"All right," he said with a smirk. "And you shouldn't be burdened by the constant weight you've placed on your back."

It took a moment for his words to sink in. All that time I had been worrying about Roy, yet unknowingly, concern for his sanity wasn't the real fear. Questioning when he'd be committed to the psychiatric hospital or if he'd crack up in jail was a case of projecting my personal fears. The deaths of Tarini and Grant unleashed in me a feeling of instability that I had previously concealed. If something were also to happen to Roy, then I might have been the next domino to fall. The thought of Roy in jail was flipping me out, and if it had gone on any longer, perhaps I would have ended up on the psych ward. After my father died, the emotional foundation he had once carefully built for me disintegrated. While I summoned his parental advice frequently, his unoriginal sayings were far from the essence of who he was. I had deliberately buried almost all memories of him and transported that trauma to a place outside my consciousness.

Re-centering and reclaiming my mental health would be an

ongoing process. I tried changing the topic, but couldn't escape the elephant in the car.

"With this special gift of yours… "

Roy cut me off with snorts and giggles. "I can't predict the future; it was only a hunch, dude. I get these weird hunches all the time. They don't mean anything. Like right now . . . I know it sounds crazy, but right now I feel like your dad is in the car with us."

"What the hell are you saying? My father is dead."

"I know. That's why it's crazy. See, my predictions and feelings are not always accurate."

The purpose of our trip to Tillamook was to bust Roy out of jail. On the trip back to Portland, Roy's words were the key to releasing my father, who still was incarcerated behind bars formed by the bones of my skull.

Some people have told me that the deceased can seem closer after they die; it was a sensation I unexpectedly encountered. Blocking out my father's death was to my detriment and, for the first time since his death, I allowed us to re-unite. The compass he had provided was still needed to guide my life. My parents had constructed and instructed me, and would always be there for me in life and after. Maybe that's what angels are. Memories of people stuck in our consciousness after death.

The more I contemplated that belief, the more I became obsessed by a strange coincidence. Tarini had died via injection above the dentate line. I felt saved by liberating the dentate section of my brain. The dentate gyrus is an anatomical segment of our lower brain responsible for recollection and navigation. In Alzheimer's dementia, it is routinely one of the first areas damaged. Once that happens, memory loss progresses, and with it, eventual deterioration of character and values. Dementia patients can still think by means of utilizing the cortex *above the dentate* portion of the brain, but they can't accurately comprehend information once their ability to recall becomes hindered.

By forcefully repressing memories, I was short circuiting the maturing process of the man and doctor I needed to become. At first it held me back only in small ways, but later, my spirit had begun to feel impaired. Just as an amputee can have phantom limb pain, the memories I had cut out of my conscience gave me mental pain.

FORTY-EIGHT

When I got home, Karen and our German shepherd immediately sat up as I entered our bedroom.

"How's Roy?" she asked.

"He's doing just fine."

"You don't look so good yourself."

"It's been a long night. I've done a lot of thinking."

The importance of family and love had never been stronger inside of me. I put my arm around her and told her how she was someone I couldn't live without; how we needed to start thinking about taking our relationship to the next level. So many of my past relationships had ended because I couldn't see myself as a married man. So it surprised me that Karen was reluctant to tie the knot. As usual she didn't hold back her opinions.

"There are a lot of clichés about the differences between women and men. Hell, half of standup comedy is about marriage. My real fears related to men is not about your well understood fantasies of screwing two women at once, or having the twenty ESPN options on cable become more important than our relationship.

"My fear is that there is a true biological difference in how men and women love. When women fall in love it is genuine and complete. Warts and all. When a man falls in love, there's always a morsel of him that wishes his wife could be something more than she currently is. Perhaps a little better looking or a little more open to this or that. Women, however, are more inclined to accept their husbands for who they are, as long as they are treated with loving respect. Husbands get grey hair, and that's o.k. with us. Little quirks or nervous habits don't bother us. But, men look at our flaws as something we need to improve on for their happiness. If we get grey hair in our late thirties, we need to dye it, or guys will start fantasizing about younger women. You know what? My hair will grey, my breasts will sag like those tribal women in National Geographic, and I'll annoy you in hundreds of other ways. My fear of marriage is that while I'm committing to you, your commitment to me will not be as strong. I may be a head turning young woman today, but that will change, Jerry. When you're a multimillionaire doctor, a decade or two from now, who has a hot young nurse worshipping your every footstep, will you still choose me?"

That speech was typical Karen. A long rant, but she had only one point to deliver and one question to ask. She was saying - I see through you and your bullshit, and still love you. Her question was - can you afford me the same luxury?

FORTY-NINE

I slept the entire day. When Karen woke me in the early evening, she interrupted a vivid dream in which my back hair, that just started sprouting in the past year, had become a nightmare. Despite shaving it, the hair was sprouting from my skin like spaghetti spewing out of a pasta-making machine.

There is no use defending back hair. I can sometimes fathom how some women regard facial hair as sexy, but there is no defending back hair, just like there is no defending neck hair. It never, ever, is sexy. Right then and there, I knew there were only two choices. Either I needed to get laser hair removal, or get married. Once you've secured your mate, men no longer have to worry about predicaments such as back hair in the same way single guys do.

Karen ordered me to, "Wake up sleepy-head! You're going to snooze your life away."

She was correct in her assertion. I would have slept another week if she hadn't awakened me. I had emerged from a sleep so deep, it was as if I had been dead.

Extreme sleep deprivation, in addition to the physical and mental stress, had worn me out. A few more cozy moments of peace would have been welcome, but Karen had made other plans.

"Get dressed. In celebration of Roy's freedom, we are all going out to dinner at Genoa, and you're buying."

Genoa was the best restaurant in a city well known for incredible cuisine. Shaving and dressing up for a big night out wouldn't have been my first choice for how to spend that evening, but the thought of some of the most delicious, creative Italian food this side of heaven provided incentive. Besides, Earl and I had narrowly escaped having to groom ourselves to face the Oregon Medical Board or court, and that was worth a grand celebration.

"Who's going with us?"

"Everybody. Earl, Roy, your mother, me, and your new friend Frankie. Oh yeah, Earl said he's bringing a date. Some girl named Savannah."

"Seriously? It just doesn't seem quite like the same old crew, does it?"

"With all your talk about the future this morning, Jerry, it's time to start living it. You're right that Tarini and Grant won't be there. The same old crew is a thing of the past. Consider it practice for old age. Someday when we're in a nursing home, as our friends die off, we'll constantly need to find new people to eat with in the dining hall."

"Very uplifting vision you have of our future."

"Forget the future, it always comes soon enough. Tonight we'll live in the present."

"I'm happy to hear this talk about you growing old with me. I guess you're giving it more thought."

"I'm still a girl, Jerry. A girl never gets her mind off her man."

Between the appetizers, Earl excused himself to go the bathroom. I did the same, since there were some questions I had for his ears only.

When Earl saw me walk into the bathroom, he asked, "How are you and Karen holding up through all this?"

"Just fine. It's been tough for everybody, but you know that."

"You treat that Karen real nice now," Earl told me. "She's got that rare combo. Not only is she good looking, she doesn't need any adjustment to her personality. I've dated too many women needing adjustment, but you can't adjust a woman. Hear me out on this one, Jerry. I've broken Mustangs and wild-eyed Arabians, but never have changed the ways of a woman. A man must recognize when a flawless thoroughbred is in his mitts. Because, when it happens, you're a lucky son of a bitch, and lightning doesn't always strike twice."

"I think you're right. Hey, don't you think Sperelakis will be coming after us? He's got revenge in his blood. Roy didn't do a tenth of the things we did to him."

Earl laughed. A kind of roar that could be heard by neighbors two houses away. I hadn't heard Earl laugh like that since the dinner party, and it reassured me that good times were around the corner.

"That's why you came to watch me take a piss?" Earl asked with a smile. He started poking me in the chest. "You don't know anything about small towns, do you? The man has been shamed. He probably didn't even stick around Tillamook to sign his resignation papers. He'll never press charges because he could never confront all the people he knows in the county legal system with the details. Sperelakis will run like a scalded dog out of that place. Besides, he'd only get into more trouble if he started an outside investigation and the facts did come out. We got a sheriff, two doctors, and a taped confession. We ain't got shit to worry about, believe me. Now excuse me, while I go spend the rest of dinner staring at the wonderful cleavage my date is kindly exhibiting for me."

Dinner was fun. To our delight, Roy seemed mostly unscathed from his ordeal. Karen did her best to crack jokes and make him chuckle, until he pleaded, "Stop making me laugh so hard, or I'm gonna vomit all this good food that I can't pronounce correctly."

Mother and Frankie got along particularly well. The memory of her deceased husband didn't constrain her from having a splendid time, and I took it as a cue that I also needed to welcome more pleasure into my life. Frankie complained that the chef didn't use enough garlic for the food to be called genuine Italian, but also remarked it was the best time he had in years.

Savannah talked about her hobbies, tanning and online poker, while Earl kept quieter than usual. He knew the more he talked, the further he'd ruin his chances with her. As usual, beads of sweat kept forming on his forehead with each bite of hot food. Karen kept to her word about sticking me with the bill, and I gladly signed for it.

The next day Frankie told me he was selling the house in Vegas. He was coming back to Portland to live, he said, and we would be seeing him frequently. Also the next day, The Oregonian reported that Sperelakis had been found 'in highly unbefitting circumstances by the church congregation,' and he indeed immediately resigned.

FIFTY

One of the most fascinating lessons life teaches is that the worst experiences can alter a person for the better.

A few months after the dinner at Genoa, life pretty much returned to normal. Earl and I made peace with our colleagues who covered our heavy patient loads during the hoopla. As in any medical practice, that meant paying back all the hours they filled in for us. The routine pattern of work was remedial for us. Winter slowly rolled into spring, and the rain stopped. The roses bloomed in the Rose City. The vitality of a new season helped wash away the death and despair. An uneventful summer gave way to fall. Nature always changes, and all living things take their cue from nature.

It was early November, and our limo traveled through a Mexican neighborhood on the way to the synagogue. Latinos were celebrating the annual Día de los Muertos, or what gringos call The Day of the Dead. The newspaper had an article that morning describing it as a festival in which the souls of deceased relatives are welcomed back for a day of remembrance, honor, and the recognition that everyone eventually dies. Día de Los Muertos, observed since the time of the ancient Aztecs, ritualizes the continuity of life. Our own Memorial Day in the United States falls short in comparison. We rarely utilize the day to recognize fallen veterans, let alone hold sacred a day for all of our departed relatives. Our commemoration consists of getting a day off work to enjoy store-wide sales, followed by a barbecue with any acquaintance willing to spring for a keg.

Earl sat to the right of me in the limo. We made small talk about how nice it would have been if Grant had been there to share in the joy of the imminent ceremony. Then he asked, "What was the last thing Grant said to you?"

I remembered the words well. "Indeed, better will come."

"Interesting," uttered Earl. "You know what he told me? That Tarini was convinced she couldn't be going to a better place. Apparently, Tarini mentioned how much she loved her friends, and that without us in it, there couldn't possibly be a heaven. Grant didn't want her to be lonely wherever she was going. I believe his suicide was more out of love than desperation. Those that claim suicide is always a selfish act have no understanding of how complex things can get."

Some of those complexities didn't have to exist for Grant. If Tarini had had complete legal autonomy in dealing with her impending fate, outcomes could have been different. The theme of our conversation nudged a tender spot that continually vexed me. Questions that at times have fundamentally changed my approach to the terminally ill. Controversies society prefers to ignore. Is it more loving to help one endure suffering, or more loving to end it? Once in a while, there can be another face of murder.

In the years that followed, we never again discussed the deaths of Grant or Tarini. A venerable seal closed the matter. To disturb that would only unlock problems nobody welcomed.

A few blocks from the synagogue our limo was nearly sideswiped by a minivan that ran a red light. Many have said that they see their entire life flash before them in near death experiences. That didn't happen for me, but the rest of the day would be filled with retrospection. A wedding may not be a near death experience, but it forces one to think a lot about the past and the future. When the Rabbi started into the vows, it provoked powerful emotions of remorse, happiness, and particularly responsibility.

In sickness and in health. Already half of Americans divorce despite good health. Sickness is not a trivial burden, as recent events had verified.

The rabbi continued the vows. *For richer or poorer.* Karen already explained her fears of men not upholding their end of the bargain in marriage, but men have the same fears. Would she have been as committed to me if I weren't a successful professional? Would she love me if I sold shirts at the Gap?

Till death do us part. That's a scary one for everybody. That is a vow of extreme pain. Unless we die in a mutually shared trauma together, such as a car crash, one will always die before the other. The torment the surviving spouse feels must be tremendous. You build a life together and suddenly it's shattered. Furthermore, agreeing to *till death do us part* has troubling implications. The best case scenario for marriage is that you will grow very old together and then never experience the sensation of falling in love with another person again.

With each reply of *I do,* the joy and fear in my heart grew stronger. Life gets a little weirder with every commitment, whether they are commitments to friends like Earl, Grant, or my soul-mate Karen. These are the major challenges in a life where only three things are absolutely guaranteed. The first two are birth and death. The third, which nobody escapes, is the experience of pain. We all feel it, and we all cause it. Joy is not guaranteed, even though the majority of us have at least some joy in our lives. Pain is unavoidable. That becomes the big question. How much pain am I willing to give Karen? As a man, I'll never one hundred percent fulfill her needs. She is also correct that I won't be one hundred percent satisfied with her no matter how much I try to dupe myself. I can't even come close to entirely satisfying my needs, let alone expect another person to do that for me.

It was a surreal experience to be standing in a synagogue thinking how the craziness of all those recent events led to my mother getting remarried. If my friends hadn't died, my mother wouldn't have taken the emergency flight to 'comfort her son' in Portland. If Roy hadn't been set up on drug charges, I wouldn't have seen Frankie Russo again. Somehow I would have to come to grips with the fact that Frankie Russo was my new stepfather. He always did call me *son* even before it became official. My mother would need to come to grips with the fact that she got married for the second time, and I wasn't yet married for the first time.

Nevertheless, despite her continued worries about me, that was the day I knew the phone calls from her would abate. Not because Frankie would request it, but rather because Frankie was the closeness she had been calling out for.

The reason for my always answering her calls was much bigger than simply an attempt to ease her mind, which was also not my mother's paramount reason for calling. Time creates spaces. The longer I was away from her, the further the distance became. With every phone call, the distance unraveled at a slower speed. Leaving for school and then subsequently moving across the country widened the canyon created by dad's death. Neither of us desired that. Thus, by answering her calls, I enabled both of us.

Frankie now provides Mother with close companionship, which is something only I was previously capable of doing. The savings on my cellular bill are enough to cover a monthly dinner at Genoa. But since the newlyweds have moved just a mile down the road, I'm considering having my doorbell chime modified to Beethoven's Fifth.

Gil Porat

ACKNOWLEDGEMENTS

It would be impossible to overstate the help my mother had in completing this book. Without her perpetual editing, it simply wouldn't have been published. The revitalizing faith of Kathleen Palmer, Armando Benitez, and Alondra Press in this project will forever be sincerely appreciated. Special thanks are also due to all Jewish mothers (not just my Jewish mother from Jersey), Southerners, my obsessive compulsion, water, logical confusion, Oregon, literature junkies, the elemental table – particularly oxygen - and all my teachers (even the ones that only taught me a little).

While writing, I often listened to Bob Dylan, B.B. King, the Grateful Dead, Etta James, Howard Stern, The Young Turks, This American Life, Franti & Spearhead, Herbie Hancock, and countless others who provided momentum to my typing fingers. Thanks for providing the soundtracks of my life.

To my wife, who appreciates the fact that writing is my therapy - thank you, and my love for you is brobdingnagian. My children, have profoundly changed my life for the better, and are the reason I care about the future of healthcare and the world.

I'm indebted to the works and teachings of Ira Byock, Dan Gilden, Jocelyn White, Timothy Quill, and definitely Eric Marcus (whose book *Why Suicide?* should be required reading). Thank you to my patients, who always enlighten and nurture me each day. I'm also grateful to Keenan and Troy for sharing their zany adventures.

To my readers who recommend this book to others, I'm indebted to you for keeping my thoughts alive.

Gil Porat